# Enid Blyton

# Treasury of Bedtime Stories

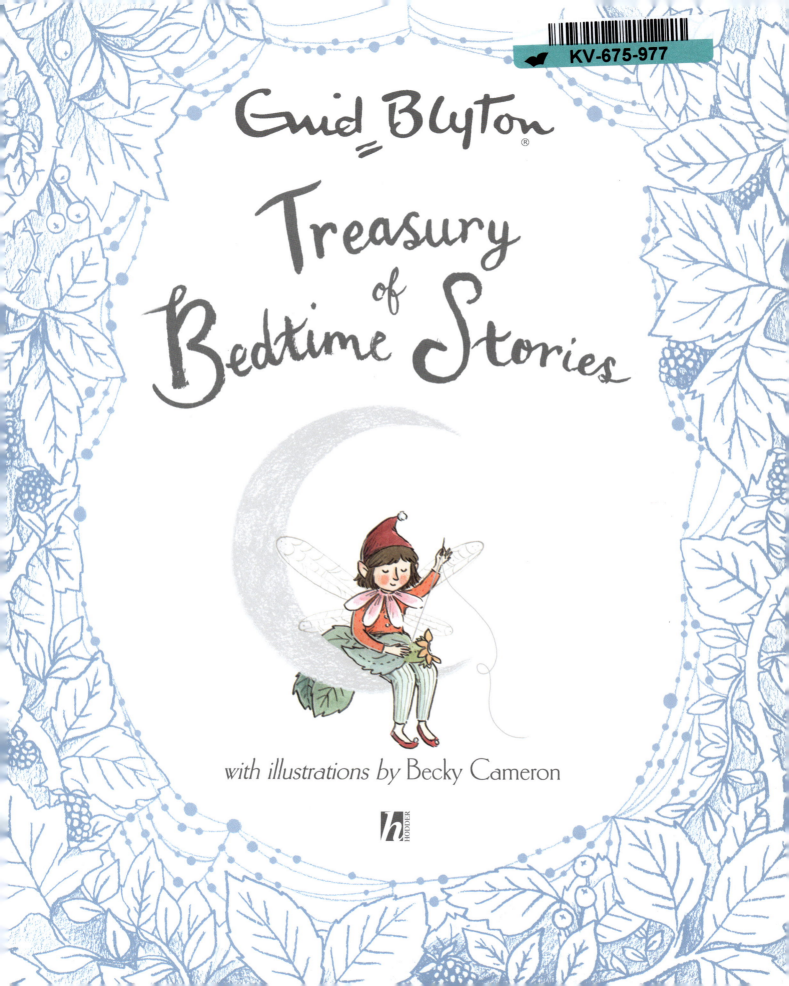

with illustrations by Becky Cameron

HODDER

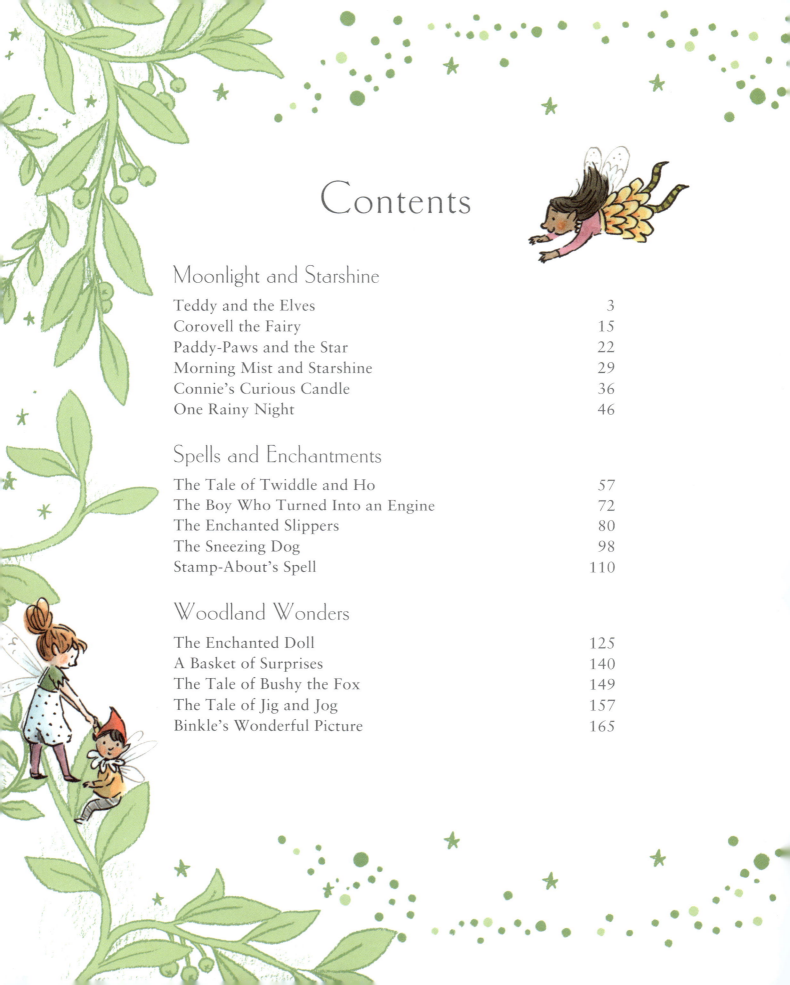

# Contents

# Treasury of Bedtime Stories

HODDER CHILDREN'S BOOKS

First published in Great Britain in 2018 by Hodder & Stoughton

5 7 9 10 8 6 4

A CIP catalogue record for this book is available from the British Library.

ISBN 978 1 444 93994 1

Typeset in Adobe Garamond by Avon DataSet Ltd,
Bidford-on-Avon, Warwickshire

Printed and bound in China

The paper and board used in this book
are made from wood from responsible sources.

Hodder Children's Books
An imprint of Hachette Children's Group
Part of Hodder & Stoughton
Carmelite House
50 Victoria Embankment
London EC4Y 0DZ

An Hachette UK Company
www.hachette.co.uk
www.hachettechildrens.co.uk

## Fairyland Folk

## Faraway Lands

# Moonlight and Starshine

# TEDDY AND THE ELVES

THERE was a new radio in the playroom. It had only just arrived, and the children were very excited about it. They had never had a radio before.

'You just press this button here to turn it on,' Emma explained to her little brother John. She pressed the round, red button on the front. There was a little click and, to the great astonishment of the toys who were listening, a band started to play. Teddy stared at the radio in surprise. The rag doll

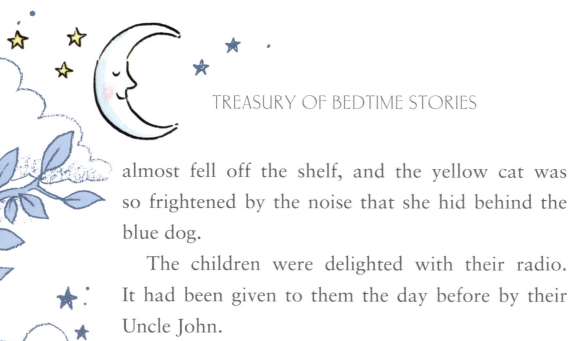

almost fell off the shelf, and the yellow cat was so frightened by the noise that she hid behind the blue dog.

The children were delighted with their radio. It had been given to them the day before by their Uncle John.

'May Emma and I keep it on, Mummy?' asked John.

'Yes – but not too loudly,' said his mother. 'And make sure you keep it somewhere safe,' she added. 'I had a nice little radio that I kept on the shelf in the kitchen and it has completely disappeared. So has my best blue and white eggcup, *and* some of my silver spoons. You haven't seen them, have you, children? I can't think where they can have gone.'

But the children weren't listening to their mother. They were busy twiddling the knob on the front of the radio instead, to see what different music they could find.

The toys thought the radio was wonderful. They listened to it all that day and all the next, and so did the children. They heard all sorts of different music and sometimes people even spoke out of the radio. The toys simply could not understand how they got in there. At other times, someone played the piano, and that seemed amazing too. How could a piano get inside such a small thing?

At night, when the children had gone to bed, the teddy bear looked longingly at the radio.

'It's magic,' he said to the others. 'It must be magic. How else can it have all those people inside it? I wish I could open it up and see exactly what is in there. How do you suppose you open it, Rag Doll?'

'Don't even *think* of such a thing!' cried the rag doll in horror. 'You might break it.'

'No I won't,' said Teddy, and he began to undo a screw at the back. The rag doll had to get the big sailor doll to come and help stop him.

'We shall put you inside the brick box, if you don't solemnly promise to leave the radio alone from now on,' said the rag doll. Teddy didn't want to be put into the brick box, so he had to promise.

But the next night Teddy wanted to press the red

button that made the radio play. 'I want to see the light come on, and hear the music play,' he said. '*Please* let me press the button!'

'What! And wake up everyone in the house and have them rushing in here to see what's going on?' cried Rag Doll. 'You must be mad.'

'But they wouldn't hear it,' said the teddy bear. 'Oh, do let me try. I promise to keep it quiet.'

'You really are a very, very naughty teddy,' said the rag doll. 'You are *not* to press that button at all.'

For the next two nights the teddy bear was quite good. But on the next night he waited until the toys were playing quietly in the other corner of the room, then he crept over to the radio and pressed the button. The light shone inside and loud music began to play!

The toys were horrified! Clockwork Clown and Sailor Doll rushed over at once and pressed the button again. The light went out and the music stopped.

'Teddy! How naughty of you!' cried the sailor doll. 'If you're not careful you will wake up the whole family. If they catch us, we will never be able to come to life at night again!'

But Teddy didn't care. 'They wouldn't have heard it,' said Teddy. 'It is you, with your big shouting voice, that will wake everyone up!'

And he ran off into the corner, squeezed himself under the children's piano, and refused to come out.

After that, Teddy wouldn't speak to any of the others, not even the little clockwork mouse who loved to chatter to him. It was very sad. Soon nobody asked him to join in the games, and the teddy bear began to feel very lonely indeed.

Deep down, Teddy knew that he should apologise to the sailor doll, and to all the other toys. But he was a proud teddy bear and he could not bring himself to say sorry.

Then one night, when the moon shone brightly outside the playroom window, Teddy could stand it no longer. He tried to join in with a game that the toys were playing, but they just ignored him.

Teddy was very upset. He walked away.

'Very well!' he called over his shoulder. 'If you

won't play with me, I'm going to find somewhere else to live!'

Out of the playroom door he went. The toys stared after him in horror. No toy ever went out of the playroom at night. Whatever was Teddy thinking of?

The moon shone brightly, and the teddy bear could see quite plainly where he was going. He went down the stairs, jumping them one at a time. They seemed very steep! He reached the bottom and looked around. Emma had sometimes taken him downstairs. He knew there was a room called the kitchen that had a nice smell in it. Which way was it?

Teddy found the kitchen door and squeezed round it. He was just about to cross the room when a shadow fell across the moonlit floor. Teddy looked up in surprise. Had the moon gone behind a cloud?

No, it hadn't. It was somebody on the windowsill, blocking out the moon – and that somebody was climbing in the kitchen window! The teddy bear stared in surprise. Who could it be, coming in through the kitchen window in the middle of the night?

*It must be a robber!* thought Teddy in dismay. *They come in the night sometimes, and steal things. Oh, whatever shall I do? The toys will be even more cross with me if I make a noise and wake everyone up. Oh dear, oh dear, oh dear!*

Meanwhile, do you know who it was climbing in through the window? Why, it was three naughty little elves. They sprang quietly to the floor, and were busy trying to open the larder door.

Usually they only came to the kitchen looking for bits of food – a slice of currant cake, perhaps, or some biscuits. But sometimes, when they were feeling very naughty, they took other things too.

Only the week before they had taken some things from one of the kitchen shelves and hidden them in the garden, but tonight they had only come to look for things to eat. Teddy watched as they started to fill their little knapsacks with food – sticky buns, pieces of cheese and even some of Emma's favourite sweets.

Then one of the elves jumped up on to a shelf and started to pick up all sorts of other things for his sack – paperclips, a little key, a coloured crayon. Then he held something up that sparkled in the moonlight.

'Hallo!' he said. 'Look what I've found!' Teddy was dismayed to see that the elf was holding a beautiful ring, which he quickly put into his sack.

*It must belong to Emma's mother*, thought Teddy to himself. *She will be so sad to lose it.*

And right there and then he decided that something must be done. So while the elves were still busy filling their sacks, Teddy slipped out of the kitchen and hurried upstairs as fast as he could go.

When he reached the playroom, he rushed through the door, panting. The toys looked at him in amazement.

'What's the matter? You look quite pale!' said the panda.

'Quick! Quick! There are three elves downstairs taking things from the kitchen!' cried the teddy. 'We must stop them. Let's wake the humans up! Come on, make a noise, everyone!'

All at once the toys started shouting. The panda growled as loudly as he could. The jack-in-the-box jumped up and down and banged his box on the floor. The toy mouse squeaked. But it was no good. No one could hear them.

No one woke up. Not a sound could be heard.

And then Teddy did a most peculiar thing! He gave a little cry, and rushed over to the radio. Before the toys could stop him, he pressed the little red button – and then he turned one of the knobs right round as far as it would go! The light went on inside the radio and a tremendous noise came blaring forth!

It was a man's voice, telling the midnight news; but the teddy bear had put the radio on so loudly that it was as if the man was shouting at the top of his voice.

'This will wake them up!' said Teddy.

And so it did! It also frightened the elves in the kitchen so much that they dropped the contents of their knapsacks all over the floor and made a terrible noise trying to scramble out of the window.

By the time Emma's father had got to the kitchen, they had quite gone.

'Must be those mice again!' sighed Emma's father, staring at the mess on the floor. Then something shiny caught his eye and he was surprised to find a

ring lying among the crumbs . . .

Upstairs in the playroom, Emma and John were turning off the radio.

'This is what woke us up, Daddy,' said John when his father appeared. 'The playroom radio. But who could have put it on?'

Nobody knew. But Emma caught a gleam in Teddy's eye as he sat by the toy cupboard. Could *he* possibly have turned on the radio? Emma knew quite well she had put him back into the toy cupboard that evening – and there he was, sitting outside it! If she hadn't been old enough to know that toys can't walk and talk, she would have felt sure he had been up to something!

'The elves have gone! They won't come back after that fright!' cried the toys once everyone had gone back to bed. 'Good old Teddy! *What* a noise the radio made, didn't it?'

Teddy was delighted to find himself such a hero. He beamed all over his face.

'Perhaps we can all be friends again now,' he said hopefully.

'Oh, yes let's!' cried all the toys together. 'It's so much nicer.'

'And perhaps every so often you'll let me turn the radio on at night *ever* so quietly,' added Teddy smiling.

'All right,' said the sailor doll. 'You deserve a reward, Teddy. You really were very clever.'

Everyone agreed. And now when he feels like listening to a little music, the teddy bear turns the radio knob – very gently – and the music comes whispering out. Emma and John *will* be surprised if they hear it, won't they?

# Corovell the Fairy

ONCE upon a time, long, long ago, the world became so full of exciting happenings that the children could not go to sleep at night. Mothers and fathers began to get worried. The fairies too were anxious, for when a child did not sleep he became cross and tired, and, of course, could not see any fairies. And the fairies did not like that at all, for they loved playing with the children.

So the king of the fairies called a great meeting,

to which all the fairies, big and little, came.

'I will offer a reward,' said the king, 'to any fairy who can find something to make all the children go to sleep at the proper time.'

All the fairies were very excited and they began to make plans at once.

'I know what I shall do,' said one. 'I shall string some baby stars together, and hold them in front of the children's eyes. They will be so dazzled with starshine that they will fall asleep at once!'

'I don't think much of that idea,' said another fairy. 'I'm going to hunt up the magic words in an old book and make them into a sleep-song. Then I shall sing it, and all the children will go to sleep, listening.'

Each fairy had a different idea, and each began to try to do what he had planned. The necklace of baby stars was no use, for the brightness made the children more awake than ever. The magic sleep-song *did* send some of them to sleep, but it kept others awake.

Another fairy tried stroking the children's hair very softly; but while it brought sleep to some, it fidgeted others. Others danced softly round the candle in the children's bedrooms, but the children were so interested in watching the fairies that they were wider awake than ever.

The fairies began to feel there was really *nothing* to be done, and one by one they gave up trying. Great gloom settled over Fairyland, for the tired children were much too cross ever to play with the fairies in the daytime.

Now all this time there was one little fairy, called Corovell, who was very busy indeed. All one day he was scraping the bloom off the darkest red roses he could find in Fairyland, and shaking it down into a yellow sack he was carrying. On another day he went to all the blue butterflies he knew, and begged them each to give him a little powder from one of their wings. Because they liked little Corovell, they shook some of their powder into his outstretched hands, and flew off into the sunshine. Corovell carefully mixed it with the rose bloom in his sack.

The next morning he scraped the sunshine from the top of all the little puddles shining in the sun.

This he mixed carefully with some black powder from the middle of bright red poppies.

He took the softest and brightest green moss growing on the palace wall, and powdered it into tiny, tiny pieces. Then he mixed into it the magic scent of the June wild roses, and shook it all up together with the other powders and dust. As he was carrying the sack along through the wood that night he picked out a star shining in a puddle and put it into his sack, just for luck. To finish off, he stirred it all up well with the brightest green feather from a kingfisher's breast.

When Corovell was satisfied with his mixture, he took his yellow sack on his shoulders and went to the king's palace.

'Your Majesty,' he said, bowing low, 'I have discovered something that will make any child sleepy.'

'Prove it,' said the king eagerly.

Corovell flew to a nursery full of naughty, tired children.

'Now watch,' he said softly. He dipped his hand

into his sack, and pulling out a handful of glittering dust, he flung some of it into each child's eyes.

The baby child fell asleep at once. The next smallest crept over to her mother and, laying her head down, went to sleep. All the other children

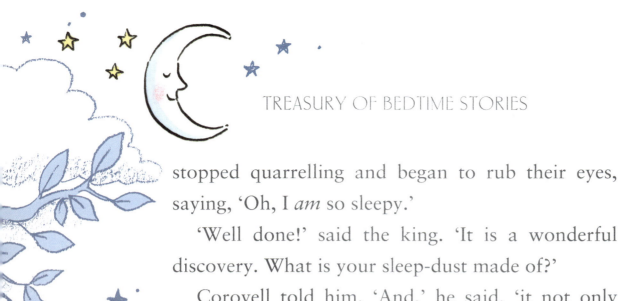

stopped quarrelling and began to rub their eyes, saying, 'Oh, I *am* so sleepy.'

'Well done!' said the king. 'It is a wonderful discovery. What is your sleep-dust made of?'

Corovell told him. 'And,' he said, 'it not only makes the children go to sleep, but it makes them dream of roses and butterflies and poppies and starshine – all the beautiful things in the world.'

'Splendid!' cried the king. 'The children will soon be happy in the daytime now, so that we can play with them again. What will you have for your reward?'

'Make me the children's Dust-man,' asked the little fairy, kneeling down before the king. 'Grant that I may be their special night-time friend, and that they may all know and love me.'

'Very well, that shall be your reward,' answered the king. 'You shall be the children's Dust-man, and make the children sleepy at night-time, so that the next day they will not be too tired to see us when we come to play with them.'

And every night since then, as quick as the gleam

on a dragonfly's wing, along comes the Dust-man with his yellow sack of magic sleep-dust. He flings some of it into every child's eyes, and they grow sleepier and sleepier, and at last fall softly asleep, to dream of flowers and birds, butterflies and starshine, until daytime peeps in through the window.

# Paddy-Paws and the Star

ONE night Paddy-Paws the rabbit was looking at the sky when he saw a shooting star. It rushed down the sky, and made a long bright trail. Then it vanished.

Paddy-Paws was astonished. He had never seen such a thing before.

'Whiskers and tails!' he said. 'That was a star falling! The moon will fall next, and then what a to-do there'll be. And oh, my goodness – if that isn't the star under the hedge!'

He looked in fright at something that shone in the hedge. He felt quite certain that it was the fallen star. Dear me, what a surprising thing!

'I must go and tell Velvet-Coat the mole,' said Paddy-Paws. So off he went to where Velvet-Coat was throwing up a big mound of earth.

'I say, Velvet-Coat,' said Paddy-Paws. 'What do you think has happened? Why, a star has fallen from the sky, and it's under the hawthorn hedge at this very moment. I saw it there!'

'Good gracious!' cried Velvet-Coat in astonishment. 'Is it really so? Let's go and tell Prickles the hedgehog.'

So off they went to where Prickles was curled up in a spiky ball.

'I say, Prickles,' said Paddy-Paws, 'what do you think has happened? Why, a star has fallen from the sky and it's under the hawthorn hedge at this very moment. I saw it there!'

'Goodness gracious!' said Prickles, uncurling himself in surprise. 'Is that really so? Let's go

and tell Bushy the squirrel!'

So off they went to where Bushy was looking for seeds in a pine cone.

'I say, Bushy,' said Paddy-Paws, 'what do you think has happened? Why, a star has fallen from the sky, and it's under the hawthorn hedge at this very moment. I saw it there.'

'Oh my, oh my!' said Bushy, dropping the pine cone in his surprise. 'Is that really so? Let's go and tell Sharp-Eyes the fox.'

So off they went to where Sharp-Eyes the fox was cleaning his fur with his tongue.

'I say, Sharp-Eyes,' said Paddy-Paws, keeping a good distance from the fox. 'What do you think has happened? Why, a star has fallen from the sky, and it's under the hawthorn hedge at this very moment. I saw it there!'

'Tails and whiskers!' said Sharp-Eyes in surprise. 'Is that really so? Let's go and tell Brock the badger.'

So off they went to find Brock, but he was far away on the hillside, and it was some time before he came to his burrow again. He found all the animals sitting outside waiting for him.

'I say, Brock,' said Paddy-Paws, 'what do you think has happened? Why, a star has fallen from the sky, and it's under the hawthorn hedge at this very moment. I saw it there!'

'What a very surprising thing!' said Brock, most astonished. 'Let us go and see it.'

So Paddy-Paws the rabbit, Velvet-Coat the mole, Prickles the hedgehog, Bushy the squirrel, Sharp-Eyes the fox and Brock the badger all went to see the fallen star under the hawthorn hedge. There it shone, all by itself.

'Look at that!' said the animals, and they sat down at a little distance from it.

'Go and get it,' said Sharp-Eyes to Paddy-Paws.

'I'm afraid,' said Paddy-Paws.

'So am I,' said Velvet-Coat.

'I daren't go near it,' said Prickles.

'Nor dare I,' said Bushy.

'Well, I'm not afraid!' said Brock the badger, and he got up to get the star. And at that very moment it moved! Only a little way, but it moved!

'Ooh! Oooh!' cried all the animals, and they scuttled away as fast as ever they could go. Paddy-Paws went to his burrow, Velvet-Coat vanished underground too, Prickles hid himself in a ditch, Bushy ran up a tree, Sharp-Eyes ran to his lair, and Brock lumbered away to his hillside. None of them wanted to touch the fallen star.

When they had all gone, a little tinkling laugh rang out in the hedge, and a small elf leapt down to the star.

'Oh, how funny!' she cried. 'They're all afraid of you, little glow-worm! They think you're a fallen star! You're not, are you! You're just a dear little glow-worm, shining in the night. I'm not afraid of you!'

She picked it up, and popped it into her lantern to light her way through the dark wood – and next morning when all the animals came to see what the star looked like in the daytime, it was gone!

'Where's it gone to?' said Paddy-Paws.

'Back to the sky!' said Brock the badger. And none of them could think why an elf nearby laughed so loudly at them!

# Morning Mist and Starshine

'I WANT that dress most particularly for Wednesday night,' said the fairy queen to Sylfai, the fairy dressmaker.

'Yes, Your Majesty,' answered Sylfai, sewing busily.

'What should you like in return for making me such a lovely dress?' asked the queen kindly. 'You can have anything you like.'

'Oh, Your Majesty, *do* you think I might come to

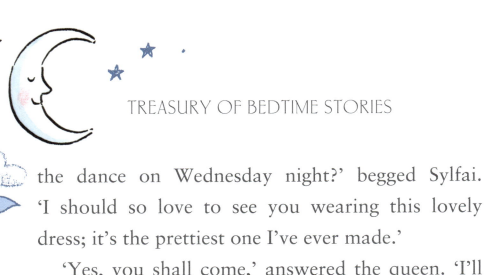

the dance on Wednesday night?' begged Sylfai. 'I should so love to see you wearing this lovely dress; it's the prettiest one I've ever made.'

'Yes, you shall come,' answered the queen. 'I'll send you an invitation; but mind, you must have on your very best dress, and you must look your very loveliest, because my cousin, the prince of Dreamland, is coming, and I want everyone to look their best.'

'Of course,' promised Sylfai. 'I'll put on all my best things, and shine up my wings beautifully.'

The fairy queen then departed, and left Sylfai happily at work. She was making a truly wonderful dress. Her thread was finest spider's web, and her stitches so small it was quite impossible to see them. The dress was made of blue morning mist and embroidered with starshine, with a little rosette of baby forget-me-not blooms at the waist. No one but Sylfai could have made it, for only she knew how to make up morning mist and starshine into dresses.

All that day she sewed, and all the next. The

rabbits came and watched her. They thought she was very clever.

'Can we do anything to help you, Sylfai?' they asked. 'Can we fetch you more spider's web?'

'Yes, please,' answered Sylfai, 'only be sure the spider has finished with it first. And when you come back, perhaps the squirrel will wind it on my reel for me.'

'Oh, yes,' said the squirrel, who loved busy little Sylfai.

But the rabbits came back saying the spiders would not give them any more silken thread.

'Nonsense!' said Sylfai, jumping up. 'You can't have told them it was for the queen's dress. I'll go and see for myself; please look after the dress for me,' and off she flew.

The rabbits and the squirrel sat round to guard the dress, but alas, the wind came by, shook the dress of morning mist as it lay on the grass, and then whisked it up into the air, and away over the tops of the trees!

'Oh dear! Oh dear!' said the rabbits.

'Oh dear! Oh dear!' sighed the squirrel.

'Oh dear! Oh dear!' sobbed Sylfai, when she came back and heard the sad news.

'Never mind,' said the squirrel hopefully. 'Tell the queen you couldn't help it, and put on your best dress and go to the dance just the same!'

'Oh, no, I couldn't,' wept Sylfai. 'I *promised* the queen she should have her dress tonight, and I'd made it so beautifully too! I shall go after the wind and see if I can get back the dress!'

Off she went, up into the air, searching all around for the frock of morning mist, but nowhere could she see it. She flew for miles and miles, and at last came to the home of the South Wind.

'Please,' she said, 'tell me where you put the dress you whisked away this morning.'

'Dear me, was it an important one?' said the South Wind.

'Yes, very. Oh, *do* tell me what you did with it,' cried Sylfai impatiently.

'Well, to tell you the truth, I don't know,' said the South Wind. 'I'm very sorry, but I never thought about it.'

'Oh dear! Oh dear!' said Sylfai sadly. 'You really *should* look what you're doing, you know.'

Off she flew again on the way home. She was very tired, and soon, to give her wings a rest, she began to walk through the wood. As she went along she heard a little frightened voice say, 'Please, could you take me home?'

Sylfai saw a tiny little fairy, whose wings were

not even properly grown.

'Well, I'm in a great hurry,' she said, 'but tell me where your home is, and I'll take you there.'

'Oh, thank you,' said the tiny fairy gratefully.

When they arrived at the birch tree where he lived, the tiny fairy's mother came out to thank Sylfai.

'Would you like to see what I found in the wood today?' she asked Sylfai. 'The South Wind brought it, and it's beautiful.' She opened a cupboard and took out something blue and shimmering.

'Oh,' gasped Sylfai in delight, 'it's the fairy queen's dress! Give it to me quickly; I may be able to get it to her in time!'

Sylfai flew along as fast as she could, hot and panting, feeling her dress torn by brambles and her hair pulled by thorns. At last, tired, dirty and torn, she arrived at the palace, and asked to see the queen. She was taken into the magnificent great hall, where everyone was assembled.

'Oh dear!' said Sylfai. 'I didn't know the party had begun! I've brought the queen's dress for her, and now it's too late!'

'Sylfai,' said the queen in great surprise, 'what do you mean by coming to my party dressed like that, and so untidy too?'

Sylfai burst into tears. Kneeling down before the queen she told all the story of the lost dress and how it was found. 'And I *didn't* mean to come to the party,' she said. 'I've only brought the dress.'

'Poor little Sylfai!' said the queen. 'You *shall* come to the party. Go and wash your face, and put on the very dress you made for *me*! Such a kind little fairy deserves the most beautiful dress in the world.'

You can just imagine how pleased Sylfai was, and everyone said that, after the queen, Sylfai looked the sweetest little fairy there, in her beautiful dress of morning mist and starshine.

# CONNIE'S CURIOUS CANDLE

THERE were four children in Connie's house. There was Philip, who was the eldest, and Helen, who was next, and George, who was seven, and then there was Connie, who was six.

There was no electric light and no gas in Connie's house. It was a very old house, and Mother used oil stoves to cook with, and oil lamps to light the rooms, and candles in candlesticks to light the bedrooms at night.

Each child had their own candlestick. Philip's was green, Helen's was red, George's was blue and Connie's was yellow. Mother used to buy coloured candles, and it was Connie's job to fit the right colours into the right candlesticks.

Every night the candles were put on the hall chest, ready for the children to carry upstairs when they went to bed. The candles used to wait there, longing for the time to come when they might wear a little yellow flame for a hat. They lit up the bedrooms then, and they could see the children getting undressed and the shadows jumping, and they could hear the prayers the children said and the creak when they jumped into bed.

One day Connie had to take the old bits of candle out of the coloured candlesticks and put in fine new candles. Mother had bought them that day – green, red, blue and yellow – one for each of the children.

'A red candle for a red candlestick,' said Connie, and she stuck the red candle firmly into the candlestick. 'A green candle for a green candlestick.

A blue candle for a blue candlestick. And here is my lovely yellow candle for my yellow candlestick. It is the prettiest of all!'

The yellow candle was pleased to hear that, but the others were not. 'Yellow is a silly colour,' said the red candle. 'Red is the best – it is the colour of warm fire!'

'No, blue is the best. It is the colour of the spring sky,' said the blue candle proudly.

'Ah, but green is the colour of the trees and the grass,' said the green candle. 'Everyone loves green.'

'Yellow is the colour of the sun,' said the yellow candle timidly. 'Surely that is a good colour?'

Nobody took any notice of the yellow candle at all, so he didn't say any more. He just longed and longed for the night to come so that he might wear his flame-hat and see the shadows jumping around him as he burnt.

But before the night came the children's mother came bustling into the hall, carrying an oil stove that she set down on the floor not far from the chest.

'It's so cold tonight I really must warm the hall,' she said to Connie. 'The hot air will rise up and warm the stairs too. It's bitterly cold today.'

The oil stove burnt clearly and sent a yellow light over the dark hall. Connie sat on the bottom stair and watched it. There was a golden pattern on the ceiling, thrown by the stove, and she liked it very much. She shivered. It was really a very cold day. She got up and went nearer to the stove, holding out her doll to warm its toes. She did not go too near, for Mother had told her that oil stoves were dangerous, and she must never go really close.

Connie looked at the candles on the chest. Her yellow one was right at the back.

'Poor yellow candle!' she said. 'You must be cold, tucked away there at the back. I'll move you forward a bit and then you will be warm.'

So she moved her yellow candle in its yellow candlestick, and placed it right at the front of the chest. It could almost see down into the oil stove! It was most exciting to watch the flame flickering up and down.

'Connie, Connie! Come out of the cold hall,' called Mother, and Connie ran into the parlour where a big fire was burning. The candles were left alone in the hall, watching the golden light from the oil stove.

Soon the yellow candle began to feel a little queer. He was hot. He felt soft. He couldn't hold his head up! He wanted to lean over to one side! It was very strange.

He did his best to stand up straight. He tried his hardest to hold firmly to the candlestick at the bottom – but he couldn't. Slowly, slowly he began to bend himself. He dropped to one side. He curled over. He grew so soft at the bottom that he seemed to be sitting on the candlestick instead of standing in it. It was dreadful!

Of course, it was the heat from the stove that was melting him! He didn't know that, and he felt very much ashamed to think he was behaving so queerly.

The other candles began to laugh at him.

'Look at Yellow!' said Red. 'He can't stand up!'

'Do you want an armchair to rest yourself in?' cried Blue cheekily.

'Poor old fellow! He's as bent over as the old man who came begging at the door today,' said Green.

'I can't help it,' said Yellow sadly in a soft, melting sort of voice. 'It isn't my fault!'

'Pull yourself together!' said Red. 'You will be no use as a candle if you stand like that!'

'How can anyone light a wick that is pointing downwards instead of up?' cried Blue. 'Why, you'd

burn yourself up at once!'

'Don't frighten me,' said Yellow sadly, and he bent himself just a little more.

'You must be a very feeble, weak sort of candle,' said Green. 'Cheap, I should think. We cost threepence each. I should think you only cost a penny.'

'I didn't!' cried poor Yellow. 'I cost threepence too!'

'Cheap candle!' cried Red, delighted.

'Penny candle!' cried Green, and he waggled his wick and laughed.

'Connie will throw you away into the dustbin when she sees what a useless candle you are!' cried Blue. 'You won't like that. You'll have to make friends with potato peel, empty tins and tea leaves!'

'Don't talk to me like that,' begged Yellow, and he wept two yellow tears of wax on to the chest.

Now very soon it was Connie's bedtime. She was the youngest, so she went first, at six o'clock. She danced out into the hall with Philip. He was ten, so he was allowed to light candles. He struck a match to light Connie's for her.

He gave a shout of surprise. 'Look! Look at Connie's candle! It's all curled over! It's no use at all!'

Red, Green and Blue chuckled to themselves, and poor Yellow wept another yellow tear on to the chest.

Mother came out into the hall. 'Oh, Connie dear!' she said. 'Did you move your candle to the edge of the chest? You have put it so near the oil stove that it has almost melted it, poor thing! It's of no use now.'

Connie looked at her candle. She couldn't bear to see it like that. 'Poor candle!' she said, almost crying. 'I only put it there to get warm. Now look what I've done to it! Poor little yellow candle!'

She began to cry. Mother picked up the candlestick and looked at the curved candle.

'Connie!' she said. 'Don't cry! This is a very clever candle! It knew it belonged to a little girl called Connie – and it has made itself into a beautiful letter

C, for Connie. Look! It's just as good a "C" as you do in your writing book!'

All the children were now in the hall, and they looked at the yellow candle. Sure enough, Mother was quite right – the candle was a big curved 'C'! Connie was simply delighted.

'Mother! Do you suppose a candle ever did that before?' she cried. 'I shall keep it always! I shall show it to all my friends!'

'Can I put *my* candle near the stove to see if it will make the letter H?' asked Helen at once.

'Oh, no,' said Mother. 'We mustn't waste candles like that. Connie, get the old candlestick from the kitchen and find yourself another candle. You may take this clever yellow one to your room and stand it on your mantelpiece!'

Well, think of that! Red, Blue and Green could hardly believe it! So Yellow was clever! Yellow was going to live on Connie's mantelpiece for a long, long time! Long after they had burnt themselves right down to the candlestick and were thrown away, the yellow candle would still stand on the mantelpiece and be admired by everyone!

'It's a mistake to laugh at people!' said Red.

So it is, isn't it? Connie's yellow candle still makes a 'C'. I'd really like you to see it.

# ONE RAINY NIGHT

ONE dark night two fairies set out to go to a party. They had on new frocks, made of buttercup petals, so the two little creatures shone as bright as gold as they ran through the night.

But they hadn't gone very far before it began to rain. They looked at one another in dismay.

'Our new frocks will be spoilt!' said Linnie.

'We shall be soaked through and tomorrow we shall sneeze and have a cold,' said Denny. They crouched under a bush and waited for it to stop. But the rain went on and on.

Presently the two fairies heard voices, and they listened. 'It's Flora's toys playing,' said Linnie. 'That means that everyone has gone to bed. Let's fly in at the window and see if they can lend us a towel to dry ourselves.'

So they flew in through the open window. The toys were very pleased to see them.

'I say! Aren't you wet?' cried the teddy bear. 'Is it raining?'

'Of course!' said Linnie. 'Did you think we had been bathing in a puddle or something?' The toys laughed. The clown went to get a towel out of the doll's-house bathroom. Soon the two fairies were rubbing themselves dry.

'Where are you going to, all dressed up in buttercup gold?' asked the curly-haired doll.

'To a party!' said Linnie. 'But it's a long way away – and we shall get wet through as soon as we fly out of the window again. It really is a nuisance. I suppose, Dolly, you haven't two old

coats you could lend us?'

The curly-haired doll got excited. 'I tell you what the straight-haired doll and I have got!' she said. 'We have each got mackintoshes and sou'westers! Flora had them in her stocking for Christmas, and we wore them when we went out in the rain. They would just fit you two!'

'Oh, do lend them to us!' begged Linnie.

So the curly-haired doll went to get them. But they were hanging up high on a peg, and none of the toys could reach them. The two fairies flew up and got them. Then they put them on, and they really did look nice in them! One mackintosh was red and the other was blue.

'I suppose it's all right borrowing them without telling Flora?' said the teddy bear. 'You know, I heard someone say the other day that nobody should ever borrow anything without asking first. And we haven't asked Flora.'

'Well, let's go and ask her then,' said Linnie.

The toys stared at her in surprise.

'We can't do that!' said the bear. 'Why, Flora

would be awfully surprised if we woke her up and spoke to her in the middle of the night!'

'But wouldn't she think it was a nice surprise?' said Denny. The toys looked at one another. The clown nodded his head.

'Yes,' he said, 'I believe she would. She is always saying that she wishes we were alive. Well, shall I go and ask her or will you, Denny and Linnie?'

'You toys had better go,' said Linnie, so all the toys went trotting across the landing to Flora's bedroom. She was fast asleep in her bed, and the bear wondered how to wake her up. He found her hand outside the sheet and patted it. She didn't wake. Then the clown tugged at the sheet, and that did wake her!

She sat up and switched on her light. She stared in astonishment at the toys. 'I must be dreaming!' she said. 'Look at all my toys standing by my bed!'

'No. You're not dreaming,' said the bear. 'We woke you up to ask you something important, Flora. There are two fairies who want to borrow the new mackintoshes and sou'westers belonging to the

dolls. It's such a rainy night and they are on their way to a party. We didn't like to lend them anything without asking first.'

'Quite right,' said Flora, getting out of bed. 'I really must see these fairies! Where are they?'

'In the playroom,' said the bear, and they all went back with Flora. She gazed in delight at the two fairies in their golden frocks and mackintoshes.

'What lovely things you are!' she said. 'Oh dear, I wonder if this is all a dream! To see my toys alive and to see fairies, all in one night, is just too good to be true!'

'Thank you for saying we may borrow these things,' said Linnie. 'We'll go now – and we'll hang them safely on the pegs when we come back!'

They flew out of the window, looking really sweet in the mackintoshes and sou'westers. The toys waved goodbye. Flora went back to bed and fell asleep again.

At cockcrow Linnie and Denny came back, after a perfectly lovely party. It was not raining now, so they could go home safely. They flew in at the

window and hung the mackintoshes and sou'westers on the pegs. The toys were all back in the toy cupboard and did not stir.

'I wish we could say thank you to Flora,' said Linnie. 'I wonder how we could.'

'I know!' cried Denny, seeing a box of letters in the cupboard. 'Look – there are lots of letters in that box! Let's spell the words "Thank you" in letters on the table. Then Flora will see them in the morning and know we have thanked her for her kindness!'

So they spelt the words 'Thank you' in letters on the table and then flew out of the window. And in the morning, when Flora came into the room, she found the words there and she stared in surprise.

'Look, Mummy!' she said. 'Isn't that funny? "Thank you." Who put it there, and why, I wonder?'

Then she went red in delight and cried out joyfully, 'Oh, I know! Of course! It was the two fairies who said thank you! Oh, Mummy, I thought last night that I dreamt my toys came to wake me up to ask me to lend two dear little fairies my dolls' mackintoshes – but it wasn't a dream after all! Dreams can't say thank you, can they?'

'I shouldn't think so,' said Flora's mother. 'Well, well, fancy you talking to toys and fairies in the middle of the night, Flora! Whatever will you do next?'

Spells and
Enchantments

# THE TALE OF TWIDDLE AND HO

ONCE upon a time there lived two pixies, Twiddle and Ho. Their cottage was at the end of Hollyhock Village, and they lived there very happily together. Every day they went to work at the pixie king's palace, not far away. It was their job to scrub the floors well, so they had to work hard, for there were many, many floors to scrub.

Twiddle and Ho got very tired of scrubbing floors, but as it was the only thing they could do really well they had to go on doing it. And then one day something happened. Wizard Humpy came to Hollyhock Village and took the cottage next door to Twiddle and Ho.

At first the pixies were frightened, for they knew that wizards were very clever. They didn't even dare to peep at Humpy, who lived quietly enough in his little cottage, and didn't bother his neighbours at all.

Strange things happened in the wizard's cottage. Often when the kitchen fire was lit, and the smoke came out of the chimney, it was bright green, instead of blue-black. Another time all the windows suddenly disappeared, and didn't come back until night-time. The cottage was nothing but walls and a door that day, for bricks grew up where the windows had been.

Then Twiddle and Ho knew that Humpy the wizard must have been doing very secret magic that day, magic that he didn't want anyone to see – so he had made all his windows vanish. It was exciting to live next door to a wizard. You never knew what was going to happen next. Once all the roses in the garden began to sing a whispering song together, and that was lovely. Another time twenty black cats appeared from somewhere to help the wizard in his magic, and that wasn't quite so nice because they miaowed so very loudly.

'It's a funny thing,' said Twiddle to Ho one day. 'It's really a very funny thing, but Humpy the wizard doesn't have anyone to do his housework or cooking for him. And yet his house always looks very clean and neat, doesn't it?'

'Yes,' said Ho, 'and we often smell simply *lovely* smells coming from his kitchen, even when he isn't there. I wonder what happens. Do you suppose he has a magic cat there that does things for him? Wizards and witches often have cats to help them.'

'I don't think so,' said Twiddle. 'But he might. Let's find out, shall we, Ho?'

So the two pixies kept a watch on the wizard's cottage. At first they couldn't find out anything. Then one night when it was very dark they stole out to peep into Humpy's windows, for they saw that he had forgotten to draw down his blinds.

And what strange sights they saw! The wizard was sitting in a cosy armchair and in front of him stood a broom, a scrubbing brush, a dishcloth and a big yellow duster. They stood up by themselves; no one was holding them. It was very strange.

The two pixies trembled with excitement. It was wonderful to see such magic. Then they heard the wizard speaking in a deep voice.

'Broom, go and sweep,' he said. 'Scrubbing brush, go and scrub. Dishcloth, wash up the supper things, and mind you don't break anything. Duster, go and dust.'

All the things bowed to him, and then they started work. You should have seen them! The broom raised clouds of dust in one corner. The scrubbing brush dipped itself in and out of a pail of soapy water and scrubbed the floor till it shone beautifully.

The dishcloth flew to the sink and began to wash up the wizard's dirty plates and dishes. It was wonderful to see it. As for the duster, it did its work really well, and even remembered to dust the tops of the pictures, a place that Twiddle and Ho

always forgot when *they* dusted!

Suddenly Humpy the wizard lifted his head and began to sniff as if he smelt something unusual. Twiddle and Ho crept quickly back to their cottage, for they guessed that he could smell pixies, and would come and look for them if they didn't go.

They looked at one another, as they sat sipping hot cocoa before going to bed.

'What strange things we have seen, Ho,' said Twiddle.

'We have indeed, Twiddle,' said Ho. 'No wonder Humpy's house is always looking spotless, if he has such willing servants! I wish *we* had some like them!'

Now two days after that the wizard shut his house up and went away. He didn't say where he was going nor how long he would be gone. He just went.

Twiddle and Ho thought of something. They both thought of the same thing, but for a long time they didn't like to say it to one another. At last Twiddle whispered it to Ho.

'Ho,' he said, 'do you suppose we could borrow the wizard's scrubbing brush until Humpy comes back? If we did, it would scrub the palace floors for us and we could have a nice rest. We could go and sit under the plum trees in the palace gardens and listen to the birds while the scrubbing brush did all our work for us!'

'That's just what I've been thinking too,' said Ho, delighted. 'Let's!'

So that night the two naughty pixies crept into the wizard's back garden, and opened the kitchen window. Twiddle slipped in and felt all around for the scrubbing brush. They didn't want anything else – only the brush.

At last he found it. It was a big brush, heavy and strong, just the sort for scrubbing wide palace floors. Twiddle was shaking with excitement when he climbed out of the window. He gave the brush to Ho to hold, and then carefully shut the window again.

Back home they went, carrying the brush. They looked at it by the light of their candle, but except that its bristles were bright blue, it seemed just the same as any other scrubbing brush. They put it in a

62

pail by the sink for the night and then went to bed.

In the morning they carried the brush to the palace and told the cook there that for once they would use their own brush, which was a very wonderful one. So the cook simply gave them their pail of soapy water and didn't bother about scrubbing brushes.

'You're to scrub the big hall this morning, and then the king's own bedroom,' said the cook. So off went Twiddle and Ho to the big hall. They set the brush on the floor and spoke to it.

'Scrubbing brush, go and scrub!' they said. 'First this big hall and then the king's own bedroom.'

To their great delight the brush at once dipped itself in the soapy water and then began to scrub the floor. You should have seen how hard it worked! The pixies stood and watched in amazement. How pleased the king would be when he saw how well his floors had been scrubbed that day!

'Now we'll go and have a nice sit-down in the garden under the plum trees,' said Twiddle. So off they went. At first they listened to the birds, but soon the hot sun made them drowsy and they nodded their small heads and fell fast asleep.

In the palace, the scrubbing brush was working hard. It scrubbed the whole of the floor of the big hall, and then it obediently went upstairs, taking the pail with it, to the king's bedroom. The carpets had been taken up ready for the floor to be scrubbed.

The brush began its work. How it scrubbed! It went into every corner and made them as clean as could be. It wasn't very long before it had finished. It sat in the pail for a few minutes, and then hopped out again. It seemed to look around for a moment or two, and then it hopped to the king's bed.

On the bed was spread a beautiful eiderdown of silver and gold, with shining flowers made of diamonds here and there. The brush began to scrub it! Dear me, what a mess it made of that fine eiderdown! The soapy water was very dirty, and very soon the eiderdown was dirty too. The brush was rough and scrubbed off many of the shining diamond flowers. Then, when it had done all it could, it looked around again.

It thought it would scrub the ceiling! Up it went and scrubbed so hard that all the lamps fell off the ceiling. Then it scrubbed the walls, and down went the pictures – crash! – on to the floor. The brush was quite mad with joy. It liked scrubbing when it could make things fall down and break. It was exciting.

The butler heard the noise and came running to see what it was. When he saw what was happening he was amazed! He watched the brush try to scrub a vase of flowers and break the glass to bits. Then he rushed over to the brush and tried to catch hold of it.

The brush rose up and hit him on the head. Crack! The butler took a step backwards and cried out in pain. The brush made a noise that sounded like a chuckle and began to scrub all the things on the king's dressing table. They flew to the floor and broke. The butler gave a loud cry of fright and rushed to the kitchen. Soon the cook came back with him and stared open-mouthed at what was happening.

'It's the magic brush those two pixies brought with them this morning!' she cried. 'The little rascals! They have left the brush to do their work and instead of staying to look after it they have gone to sit in the garden!'

The butler went to fetch Twiddle and Ho. He found them under the plum trees, fast asleep. How he shook them!

They woke with a dreadful jump, and when they heard what the butler had to say, they turned quite pale. They rushed into the palace and went to the king's bedroom. There they saw what a dreadful mess it was in, lamps, pictures and everything else on the floor, and the brush trying to scrub the bottle of medicine that the king took three times a day.

Twiddle and Ho rushed at the brush and tried to pick it up. Rap! Crack! Twiddle got a sharp rap on his knuckles, and Ho got a blow on the head. And no matter how hard they tried to get hold of that brush they couldn't – it simply hit them hard and hopped away.

'Can't you stop it scrubbing?' shouted the butler angrily. 'You started it off, didn't you? Well, stop it then!'

'Stop scrubbing!' cried Twiddle and Ho. But the brush took no notice at all. Then the pixies felt dreadful. They remembered that they hadn't heard what the wizard said to stop the brush from scrubbing, because they had crept back home before the work had been finished.

Suddenly a voice behind them made them jump in fright. It was the king, returned home from his ride.

'What's all this?' he asked in astonishment. 'Why are you all in my bedroom? And what a dreadful mess it is in!'

The butler explained what had happened – but before he had finished, the brush hopped over the floor to the king and began to scrub his boots! Then it flew to his head and began to scrub his hair!

The king was angry, and as for the two pixies, they trembled with fright. How dare the brush scrub the king himself?

The king knew a good deal of magic. He called out a few words and the brush left him. It rushed to Twiddle and Ho and began to scrub *them*! How they yelled!

'Go home and take your brush with you!' said the king sternly. 'And don't come here again. You have lost your jobs.'

Crying bitterly, the two pixies left the palace – and the brush went with them. It scrubbed them hard all the way home, and poor Twiddle had no tunic left when at last he went into his cottage. What were they to do? They didn't know *how* to stop the brush!

'If only Wizard Humpy would come home, we could go and confess and ask him to take away this hateful brush,' sobbed Twiddle. But there was no one in the wizard's cottage. He hadn't come back. So all that night Twiddle and Ho had to put up with the brush scrubbing them hard, and it was very painful indeed.

Next morning, to their great joy, they saw Humpy the wizard going into his cottage. He had come back!

At once they rushed into his garden and knocked at the door, the brush scrubbing away at their shoes all the time. Humpy opened the door and when he saw what was happening he *did* look surprised.

Twiddle and Ho told him everything.

'We are very, very sorry for what we did,' they

said. 'Please forgive us and take away your scrubbing brush.'

'I don't want it,' said Humpy. 'It's never been a really good one. I can get another. You can keep that, seeing you borrowed it.'

'But we don't want it!' cried Twiddle in a panic. 'We don't want it, Humpy. We hate it! It has spoilt all our clothes with its horrid scrubbing, and besides it is so painful to be scrubbed all day. Do take it away.'

'No, I don't want it,' said Humpy. 'It serves you right for borrowing without asking.'

'Oh, we'll do anything for you if only you'll take away this horrid brush,' sobbed Ho.

'Well,' said Humpy, 'I'll make a bargain with you. I can sell my magic broom, scrubbing brush, dishcloth and duster to Green-Eye the witch. But if I do that I shan't have anything to do my housework for me, and nobody will be servant to a wizard if they can help it. Will you come and do all my housework for me, if I take away that brush?'

'Oh, yes, yes!' cried the pixies.

So the wizard clapped his hands three times and cried, 'Brush! Go to your pail!' At once the brush left the pixies and flew to a pail under the sink, where it stayed quite quietly. How glad the pixies were!

But now they are the wizard's servants and they have to work twice as hard as they used to do. They sweep and scrub, mop and dust from morning till night, and they are very, very glad to creep home and sit down to a cup of hot cocoa before going to bed. Then they look at one another and shake their heads.

'We won't take anything that doesn't belong to us *ever* again!' says Twiddle. And I don't suppose they ever will!

# THE BOY WHO TURNED INTO AN ENGINE

THERE was once a boy called Thomas who simply loved playing at engines. He put his hands up before him to make the buffers of an engine, and then raced round the garden, puffing for all he was worth!

You could hear him any day – 'ch-ch-ch-ch-ch-ch!' Mrs Brown next door knew when he was in the garden because she could hear the 'ch-ch-ch,' and the 'ooooo' that Thomas made when he whistled like an engine.

The grocer knew when Thomas ran by each day because he too heard 'ch-ch-ch-ch' and 'oooooo'. Mrs Penny, who liked to snooze in a chair in her front garden, was often woken up with a jump when the little Thomas-engine went rushing by her gate: 'ch-ch-ch-ch.' He always gave a loud 'oooooo' just there because her house was supposed to be a tunnel.

'One day, Thomas,' said his mother, 'you will certainly turn into an engine! Couldn't you be a car for a change, or an aeroplane?'

'No, Mummy,' said Thomas. 'I love engines best. I like to pretend to be an engine all the time. Oh, how I wish I was an engine driver!'

Now one day, when the sun shone out warmly and daffodils nodded everywhere, the wind blew from the south-west. As I daresay you know, Fairyland lies to the south-west, and the wind had blown from there. And that day there was magic in the wind!

It had blown over Witch Humpy's house and she had been making spells that morning in a big pot over her fire. The steam from the pot had mixed with the green smoke that came out of her chimney and the wind had taken it to play with. It blew it here and there before it – and it so happened that it blew the magic steam and smoke over Thomas as he ran puffing 'ch-ch-ch-ch-ch' by the side of the railway track. 'Ooooooo,' shouted Thomas as he went, just like a real train coming in at the station.

'Ooooo-oo!' shouted the wind and puffed the bit of witch-smoke into Thomas's face.

And in that very moment Thomas changed into a real engine! He found himself rushing along a railway track. He was shouting 'ch-ch-ch-ch' very quickly and very loudly indeed. Thomas tried to look down at his feet to see how it was that he was going so quickly.

But he had no feet – only great wheels that tore round and round and round as he went! Thomas was so astonished that he nearly ran off the track!

*I've changed into an engine!* he thought to himself. *A real engine! However did it happen? I wonder how loud I can whistle now.*

He whistled – 'OOOOOOOOOOOOO.' My goodness, it was so loud that Thomas made himself jump. He wobbled a bit on the track and felt quite scared.

*I must be careful*, he thought. *It won't do to get off the track. There might be an accident. I wonder if I've got any carriages behind me.*

He looked to see – and to his delight he found that he had above twelve carriages in a row, all tearing after him. Just at the back of him was the coal truck full of coal. In his cab burnt a big fire and a driver and stoker stood there, talking. People sat in the carriages and read their papers. The train was going a very long way.

'Ch-ch-ch-ch-ch!' went Thomas in delight. My, it was fine to be a real train, on a real track, instead of just a pretend one going down the road. He thundered through stations, and whistled at the top of his voice, 'OOOOOOOOO!'

He ran under long, dark tunnels, and once he was very frightened to see what he thought was a big black animal with red eyes coming towards him

in a tunnel – but it was only another train going the opposite way. Thomas laughed and let off steam. It made a great chuffy noise and startled all the cows in a nearby field.

On he thundered, and on. He went over a bridge and looked down into a deep river. He stopped once at a busy station and people jumped in and out of the carriages. Thomas was quite glad of the rest. He stood there, puffing and blowing. Then he whistled again, 'OOOOOO,' and set off once more. 'Ch-ch-ch-ch-ch!' He raced through the countryside joyfully, and the driver turned to the stoker in surprise.

'My, isn't the engine going well today,' he said. 'Like a little boy running home from school!'

At last Thomas came to a seaside station. He could go no further, for the blue sea lay in front of him. He stopped and everyone got out. Thomas felt terribly thirsty. The driver ran him to a big tank and let down a hose. Thomas had a long, long drink. How delicious it was!

In a little while it was time for Thomas to start back. He saw the people getting into the carriages.

He was longing to go. He puffed impatiently – 'ch-ch-ch-ch-ch!' Then he gave a piercing whistle, and made a dog jump almost out of its skin, and a little girl began to cry!

At last Thomas was off once more. He thundered down the track, chuffing out white smoke, and whistling whenever he came to a level crossing. He shot in and out of the tunnels. He clattered over bridges and shrieked through stations, having a perfectly glorious time!

And then he came to his own station at home. And do you know, as he watched the people getting out of the carriages, he saw his own father! Yes, there he was getting out of the train to go home!

Thomas was so pleased to see him. He shouted loudly, 'Daddy! Daddy!' But his voice turned into a loud whistle, and his father didn't hear his name being called. He walked on towards the station gate.

'Daddy, look at me, I'm a real engine!' shouted Thomas, and he tried to run after his father. He got off the track – he jumped on to the platform – he rushed after his father!

But nobody seemed surprised to see an engine get off the track and on to the platform – because as soon as he left the track Thomas became himself again! He tore over the platform on two legs, his hands held up as if they were engine buffers, and came up to his father.

'Hallo, hallo, hallo!' said Father, as he heard the 'ch-ch-ch-ch!' and the loud 'oooooo!' beside him. 'Here's the little Thomas-engine again! One of these days, Thomas, you will certainly turn into an engine and go tearing down the track!'

'That's just what I have been doing today!' said Thomas. But Father only laughed. He didn't believe him at all.

So now Thomas is waiting to change into an engine again – and then he is going to jump off the railway track, go puffing down the road and up to the front door of his home. He thinks his parents will believe his tale then.

Wouldn't you love to be there when he comes chuffing up: 'ch-ch-ch-ch'? I would. What a surprise it will be to see a real train come up the garden path!

# The Enchanted Slippers

ONCE upon a time there was a boy called William, who lived with his mother at the foot of some high hills. Nobody lived up on the hills for it was said that dwarfs lived in caves there, and no one liked to walk on the sunny hillside.

William's mother often warned him not to go wandering in the hills, and to beware of any strange thing that he saw for fear it was enchanted. But William saw nothing at all, and he wasn't a bit afraid of dwarfs, no, nor giants either. Not he!

One day he went to look for wild strawberries at the foot of the hills. They were hard to find but, just as he was about to give up, he suddenly saw a sunny bank, just a little way up the hill, where he was quite certain he would find some.

To get there he had to cross a very boggy piece of ground – and dear me, before he knew what was happening he was sinking right down in it!

Quickly William slipped off his heavy boots, which were held tightly in the mud, and leapt lightly to a dry tuft of grass.

'Bother!' he cried. 'I've lost my boots! I shall get thorns and prickles in my feet if I'm not careful.'

Then he saw a strange sight – for on a dry flat stone just in front of him there was a pair of fine red slippers with silver buckles! William stared at them in surprise. Who could they belong to? He looked around but he couldn't see anyone.

'Hallo! Is anybody about?' William shouted loudly. 'Whose shoes are these?' But there was no answer at all.

William looked at the shoes again. It seemed a pity not to borrow them when he had none. He wouldn't soil them – he would just wear them home and then try to find out who the owner was.

So he picked up the shoes and slipped them on his feet. They fitted him exactly.

William thought they looked very nice. He stood up and tried them. Yes, they really might have been made for him!

*I'd better go back down the hill*, he thought suddenly. *I've come too far up, and Mother always warns me not to.*

He turned to go back down – but to his surprise his feet walked the other way! Yes, they walked *up* the hill, instead of down!

William couldn't believe it. Here he was trying to walk down the hill and he couldn't. He tried to force his feet to turn round but it was no good at all! They simply wouldn't!

'Oh, no!' said William. 'Why did I meddle with these shoes? I might have guessed they were magic! I've got to go where the shoes lead me, I suppose.

I wonder, though, if I could take them off.'

But his feet wouldn't stop walking long enough for him to try, so on he had to go. Up the hill his feet took him, along a steep path, and up to a small yellow door in the hillside.

As he came up to it, the door opened and a little dwarf, dressed in red and yellow, looked out. He grinned when he saw William.

'Ha! So my shoes have caught someone at last. Good!'

'You've no right to lay traps like that,' said William crossly, as his feet took him through the door. 'Take these shoes off my feet at once!'

'Oh, no, my fine fellow!' said the dwarf, chuckling. 'Now I've got you, I'm going to keep you. It's no good trying to get those shoes off – they're stuck on by magic, and only magic will get them off!'

'Well, what are you going to do with me?' asked William.

'I want an errand boy,' said the dwarf. 'I do lots of business with witches, wizards and giants, sending out all sorts of spells and charms – and I want

83

someone to deliver them for me.'

'I don't see why I should work for you!' said William. 'I want to go home.'

'How dare you talk to me like that!' cried the dwarf, flying into a rage. 'I'll turn you into a frog!'

'All right, all right!' said William with a sigh. 'But I shall escape as soon as I possibly can.'

'Not as long as you've got those shoes on,' said the dwarf with a grin. 'They will always bring you back to me, no matter where you go!'

Poor William. He had to start on his new job straight away!

The dwarf wrapped up a strange little blue flower in a piece of yellow paper and told William to take it to Witch Twiddle. The shoes started off at once and, puffing and panting, William climbed right to the top of the hill where he found a small cottage half tumbling down. Green smoke came from the chimney and from inside came a high chanting voice. It was the witch singing a spell.

'Come in!' she called when William knocked at the door. He went inside and found Witch Twiddle stirring a big black pot over a small fire. She was singing strings of magic words, and William stood open-mouthed, watching.

'What are you gaping at, nincompoop?' said the witch impatiently.

'I'm not a nincompoop!' exclaimed William. 'It's just that I've never seen boiling water send up green steam before!'

'Then you *are* a nincompoop!' said the witch. 'What have you come here for anyway?'

'I've come from the dwarf down the hill,' said William. 'He sent you this.'

He held out the little yellow package, and the witch pounced on it greedily.

'Ha! The spell he said he would give me! Good!'

William wanted to sit down and have a rest, but the enchanted slippers walked him out of the cottage and down the hill again.

Trimble the dwarf was waiting for him with a heap of small packages to deliver.

'Look here!' said William firmly, 'I'm not going to take all those. I want a rest.'

'Well, you'll have to do without one,' said the dwarf. 'I want these packages delivered. This goes to Cast-a-Spell the wizard, and this to Dwindle the dwarf, and this to Rumble the giant.'

'But I don't know where they live,' said William.

'That doesn't matter,' said Trimble. 'The enchanted slippers will take you there!'

And so they did. It was most peculiar. First they took him to a little wood, in the middle of which was a very high tower with no door. A neat little notice said:

CAST-A-SPELL
THE WIZARD

'That's funny,' said William, looking all around. 'There's no way to get in!'

He knocked on the wall of the tower.

'Come in, come in!' cried a voice.

'How?' asked William. 'There's no door.'

'Oh, bless me if I haven't forgotten to put the door back again!' said a grumbling voice from inside.

'Come back, door!'

At once a bright green door appeared in the tower.

William stared at it, astonished. Then he opened it and stepped into a small, round room where a hunched-up old man sat reading an enormous book. His beard was so long and thick that it spread all over the floor. William had to take care not to tread on it.

'Here you are,' said William. 'It's a parcel from Trimble the dwarf.'

William gave the old man the package and left. To his surprise the door vanished as soon as he was outside. It was most peculiar.

His enchanted slippers would not let him stay for a moment. They ran him out of the wizard's wood and took him halfway down the other side of the hill before they stopped.

'What's the matter now?' wondered William. 'I can't see any house. These slippers have made a mistake. I hope they won't keep me out here in the cold all day!'

Just then the earth began to shake beneath his feet! He felt frightened, and wondered if there was an earthquake. Then suddenly he heard a cross little voice.

'Get off my front door! I can't open it. Get off, I say!'

The voice seemed to come from down below. William felt the earth shaking under him again – and then, to his astonishment, he saw that he was standing on a neat brown trapdoor, just the colour of the hillside! On the trapdoor was a little nameplate that said:

**DWINDLE THE DWARF**

'I'm so sorry!' called William. 'I didn't know I was standing on your front door! But my feet won't get off it.'

There was an angry noise below. Then suddenly

someone pushed the trapdoor open so hard that William was sent flying into the air and fell down with a bump.

'Careful!' shouted William crossly. 'You sent me flying!'

'Serves you right,' said the bad-tempered dwarf, sticking his head out of the open trapdoor. 'What do you want here, anyway? Are you the boy that brings the potatoes?'

'No, I am *not*!' said William. 'I've been sent by Trimble the dwarf to bring you this package.'

The dwarf snatched the parcel from his hand and disappeared down the trapdoor at once, slamming it shut behind him.

'Go away,' he called. 'And don't you ever stand on my door again.'

At once William's enchanted slippers took him back up the hill at a fast trot.

'I've only got to go to Giant Rumble now,' said William. 'Thank goodness! I feel quite exhausted!'

Soon he came to something that looked like a big golden pole. As he got near it he saw that it was a long, long ladder of gold, reaching up into the sky and into a large black cloud.

His feet began to climb up the ladder, and dear me, it was very hard work! Before he was very far up he badly wanted a rest – but the enchanted slippers wouldn't stop. Up and up they went!

After a long while William reached the top. He looked round and saw an extraordinary palace, which seemed to be made entirely of mist.

'This doesn't look as if it is the home of a giant,' said William to himself. 'It's big enough – but it doesn't seem strong enough! It's all so soft and misty!'

But all the same, a giant *did* live there. The front door opened as William drew near, and inside he saw a great hall, higher than the highest tree he had ever seen. Sitting at a carved table was a giant with a broad, kindly face. He looked down smilingly at the boy as he walked forward.

'Where do you come from, boy?' he asked.

'From Trimble the dwarf,' answered William. 'He sent you this parcel.'

'About time too,' said the giant, stretching out

such an enormous hand for it that William felt quite frightened. 'Don't be afraid, my boy. I won't hurt you. I'm a cloud giant, and I live up here to make the thunder you hear sometimes. But I do no harm to anyone.'

The giant opened the parcel and then frowned angrily. 'The dwarf has sent me the wrong spell again!' he grumbled. 'Do *you* know anything about spells, boy?'

'Nothing at all,' said William.

'Dear me, that's a pity,' said Rumble. 'I'm doing a summer-thunder spell, and I've got to multiply twelve lightning flashes by eleven thunder claps. I don't know the answer. Trimble said he'd send it to me, but he hasn't, I'm sure.'

'What does he say the answer is?' asked William, who knew his tables very well indeed.

'He says that twelve flashes of lightning multiplied by eleven claps of thunder make ninety-nine storm clouds,' said Rumble.

'Quite wrong,' said William. 'Twelve times eleven is one hundred and thirty-two.'

'Well, is that so?' said the giant. 'I *am* pleased! Now I can do my spell. I'm really very much obliged to you. I suppose I can't possibly do anything for you in return?'

'Well, yes, you can,' said William at once. 'You can tell me how to get rid of these slippers.'

'Well, the only way to get rid of them is to put them on someone else,' said Rumble. 'Tell me who you'd like to put them on and I'll tell you how to get them off!'

'I'd like to make that horrid little dwarf Trimble wear them, and send him off to the moon!' said William.

'Ha, ha, ha, ha!' laughed the giant. 'Best joke I've heard for years! That would serve him right. Now listen. Wait till the dwarf is asleep, and then slip these tiny stones into your slippers. You will find that they come off at once. Put them on Trimble's feet before you can count ten, and tell him where to go. He'll go all right! The slippers will start him walking and he'll never come back.'

'Oh, thank you,' said William gratefully and took

94

the small pebbles that Rumble gave him. He said goodbye to the kindly giant and then climbed quickly down the ladder. He was soon back at Trimble's house and found him having his dinner. The dwarf threw the boy a crust dipped in gravy and told him that as soon as he had finished eating there were some more errands to do.

'I'm going to have my after-dinner nap,' he said, lying down on a sofa. 'Wake me when you've finished cleaning up.'

William was too excited even to eat his crust. As soon as he heard Trimble snoring loudly William slipped the magic pebbles into the slippers. They came off as easily as could be, and in great delight he ran over to Trimble. As soon as the slippers were off, William began to count.

'One, two, three,' he counted, as he began to slip the shoes on to Trimble's feet – but to his horror the dwarf's feet were far too large – twice the size of William's! Whatever could he do?

'Four, five, six, seven, eight, nine . . .' he continued to count in despair, for the shoes certainly would *not* go on the dwarf's feet. And then, at the very last moment, William had an idea. He would put them on the dwarf's hands! He fitted them on quickly, counting 'Ten!' as he did so – and at the same moment the dwarf awoke!

'What are you doing?' he cried angrily, jumping up. 'I'll turn you into a frog, I'll—'

'Walk to the moon!' shouted William in excitement – and then a most extraordinary thing happened! For the dwarf suddenly stood on his hands and began to walk on them out of his cottage! Trimble was even more astonished than William.

'Mercy! Mercy!' he cried. 'Take these slippers off.'

'I don't know how to,' said William. 'But anyway, it serves you right. Go on, slippers – walk to the moon and then, if the dwarf has repented of his bad ways, you may bring him back again!'

The dwarf was soon a long way off, walking upside down on his hands, weeping and wailing.

As soon as the dwarf was out of sight a crowd of little folk came running up to William. They were dressed in red and green tunics and had bright happy faces.

'We are the hill brownies,' they said, 'and we've come to thank you for punishing that horrible dwarf. Now we shall all be happy, and you and your friends can walk safely up the hillside. Ho, ho! Wasn't it a surprise for Trimble to be sent walking to the moon on his hands? That was very clever of you.'

The jolly little hill brownies took William safely back home, and even fetched his lost boots for him out of the bog into which they had sunk. And now William and his friends walk unafraid all over the hills, for the friendly brownies are about now and the nasty dwarfs have fled, frightened by the fate of Trimble.

As for Trimble, he hasn't even walked halfway to the moon yet, so goodness knows when he'll be back!

# THE SNEEZING DOG

THERE was once a dog called Collie, and, as you can guess, he was a collie dog. He lived in a yard, and he had a big kennel to himself, because he was a big dog. He was on a chain, because he had to guard his master's house, and Mr Snoot didn't want him wandering about loose, far away from the house.

So Collie was always tied up, except when Mr Snoot took him out for a walk. He was often very bored. It wasn't much fun to sit night and day inside or outside his kennel, when he wanted to go and hunt rabbits or see his friends. All he could do was to bark loudly when any stranger came to the yard.

That was what Mr Snoot wanted him to do. Mr Snoot was a miser, and he had a good deal of money hidden up his kitchen chimney. As soon as he heard Collie bark he was warned of people coming, and he could look out for them.

When the winter came Mr Snoot put more blankets on his bed. He bought extra milk from the milkman so that he could warm it up at night and put it beside his bed in a flask to keep it hot. He had a tin of his favourite biscuits there too to eat with the hot milk. He didn't mind waking up at night then, for he would pour himself out a glass of hot milk and eat a few biscuits. Then he would pop down into his kitchen, put his hand up the chimney, feel to see if his moneybag was there and go back to bed again, quite happy.

He would pull his lovely warm blankets over his head, and go peacefully to sleep, knowing that if any tramp or robber came along, Collie would bark loudly to tell him.

The days were cold. The nights were colder. Collie had some straw in his kennel to lie on, but not much, and what there was was rather flattened down by the weight of his big body. He shivered. It made his chain rattle when he shivered. He got further into his kennel and tried to spread the straw round himself, but there wasn't enough.

He went out to his bowl to get a drink, and to see if there were any biscuits left. Perhaps a meal would warm him up a bit. But alas, the water had frozen hard. His dinner bowl was quite empty.

Poor Collie! He went back into his kennel, and wished that Mr Snoot had swung it round to face the other way, because the cold north wind came blowing straight into the kennel. How could a dog possibly get warm with a wind like that blowing at him all the time?

Collie felt colder and colder. He shivered more and more. Then he felt a sneeze coming. It was a big one. *A-a-a-a-a-WHOOOOOSH-ooooo!*

sneezed Collie loudly.

There was a squeal from outside, a squeal of fright. Then a little voice said, 'What did you do that for? You blew me off my feet!'

Collie stuck his nose outside in surprise. Who was this? He hadn't heard anyone. Ought he to bark?

Outside stood a small man dressed in a brown tunic, and brown stockings and shoes. He wore a pointed hat, and had a long grey beard. His bright blue eyes twinkled like stars in a frosty night.

'Hallo!' said Collie surprised. 'One of the little folk, I suppose? What are you doing here at this time of night?'

'I got called out to a robin who's half frozen,' said the brownie. 'I'm a doctor, you know. Dr Help-a-Bit. You may have heard of me.'

'Well, I haven't really,' said Collie. 'Did I almost blow you off your feet just now when I sneezed?'

'Right off,' said Dr Help-a-Bit. 'I got an awful shock. What's the matter with you, sneezing like that? And why do you keep rattling your chain?'

'Well, brownie, I don't mean to rattle it, but I can't help it, because I'm so cold,' said Collie. 'It's my shivering that rattles the chain.'

'What a shame!' said the brownie. 'Get out of your kennel, and go and bark at the house door. They'll have to let you into the warmth then.'

'I can't,' said Collie. 'I'm chained. Can't you see? I'm terribly cold because I can't run about to keep myself warm, and I haven't enough straw to cuddle down in.'

'I can't have this sort of thing,' said Dr Help-a-Bit, looking very fierce all of a sudden. 'I'll go and see your master about it. Poor creature! How can anyone treat you like that? I'll go and wake your master.'

Before Collie could stop him the brownie had gone to the back door, opened it with a key he had, and gone inside. He went upstairs, drawn there by a loud noise of snoring. He came to Mr Snoot's bedroom. By the light of the little lamp that Mr Snoot always left burning, the brownie saw the fat old man lying fast asleep in bed.

'Wake up!' said the brownie sternly. Mr Snoot didn't stir. The brownie gave him a prod. Still Mr Snoot didn't wake. Then Dr Help-a-Bit's eyes gleamed.

He had noticed the great pile of warm, woolly blankets that Mr Snoot had on his bed. He saw the flask of hot milk by the bedside and the tin of biscuits. How pleased a cold and hungry dog would be with all those things.

The brownie put the tin of biscuits in one pocket and the flask of hot milk into another. Then, softly pulling at the pile of woolly blankets, he dragged them all off the bed, tucked them round his shoulders to carry, and went downstairs again. Mr Snoot had nothing on him except for a thin sheet. All his blankets had gone.

Dr Help-a-Bit took everything outside. 'Here you are,' he said to Collie, pouring the milk into the bowl. 'Drink it up while it's hot. And eat these biscuits – you'll like them. Then I'll pack your kennel with these fine blankets and you'll be as warm as toast, as soon as you cuddle down in them.'

Collie was overjoyed. He lapped up the hot milk. He crunched up the delicious biscuits. Then he squeezed into the fleecy blankets and the brownie pulled them closely round him. 'I'm sorry I'm not strong enough to swing your kennel away from the cold north wind,' he said. 'But I don't somehow think you'll feel the cold now!'

Collie didn't! He slept all night long in warmth and comfort, a very happy dog. How kind of the brownie to bother about him like that! Collie wished he could do something in return, but he couldn't think of anything.

Now about half an hour later, Mr Snoot awoke shivering with cold. He put out his hand and felt for his blankets. They weren't there. They must have fallen on the floor, he thought. He sat up and looked.

What a very extraordinary thing – they weren't on the floor either. In fact, they were nowhere to be seen.

Cold, puzzled and frightened, Mr Snoot took up his flask to pour out a glass of hot milk. It was empty! The brownie had carefully taken it back with the biscuit tin and put them in their place beside Mr Snoot's bed. No biscuits, no milk, no blankets! Mr Snoot was alarmed. He thought there must surely be burglars about – and yet Collie hadn't barked!

He crept downstairs and felt for his moneybag up the chimney. It was still there. He pulled it down, and dragged it upstairs. He locked the door and looked around for a bed covering. There was nothing he could use except for a tablecloth, and that wasn't very warm! So Mr Snoot shivered all night long, and couldn't sleep at all.

In the morning he went to scold Collie for letting a thief come in the night without barking at him. He saw something in Collie's kennel, and how astonished he was to find that all his blankets were stuffed there! He pulled them out in amazement.

'Who did this?' he said sternly to Collie. 'It couldn't have been you because you are always chained up. It's a very silly joke, whoever did it. I am not pleased.'

Well, as he had taken the blankets away, poor Collie was as cold as ever the next night. But along came the brownie again to see if he was all right – and how angry he was when he found that Mr Snoot had taken away the blankets, but hadn't bothered to give poor Collie any more straw – or even to give him water instead of the ice in his bowl.

'Well, Snoot can shiver all night again,' he said grimly. 'I'm going to get his blankets, his hot milk and his biscuits once more!'

So into the house he went, up the stairs and into the bedroom. Once again he pulled the blankets off the snoring Mr Snoot, and took his flask of hot milk and his biscuits. And once again Collie lapped eagerly, crunched the biscuits and then snuggled down in the blankets.

And once more poor Mr Snoot awoke shivering with the cold, and looked for the blankets that were not there! He was really very frightened when he found that they had disappeared again!

He lit a lantern, put on his dressing gown and went downstairs and out into the yard. Yes, just as he had thought, Collie had his blankets again; and what was this in his bowl? A drop of milk – and a few crumbs of his best biscuits! So that was where his things were going! Mr Snoot was angry.

He tried to pull the blankets out of Collie's kennel. But Collie held on to them, and it looked as if they would be torn to pieces!

'I *must* have my blankets!' roared Mr Snoot. 'I shall freeze at night if I don't.'

'And what about your dog, you selfish fellow?' said a stern voice nearby. Mr Snoot turned and saw the brownie looking at him. 'Hardly any straw in his bitterly cold kennel, no water to drink – shivering all night long, poor thing. You ought to be ashamed of yourself. Collie, let go of the blankets. I've an idea!'

Collie let go. Mr Snoot bent to snatch them, but the brownie took them first. He glared at Mr Snoot.

'You'll stay out here in this yard all night long, and see what it is like! I'm going to take Collie upstairs and put him into your bed and cover him with these blankets. You stay here and pretend to be him. See how you like it!'

Mr Snoot watched the brownie and Collie going indoors. Dr Help-a-Bit had undone the chain, so

Collie was free. Mr Snoot tried to go after them, but the brownie had put magic into his slippers and he couldn't move a step out of the cold, windy yard.

But Collie slept well tucked in Mr Snoot's comfortable bed. What a night he had! Mr Snoot found him there in the morning when he went upstairs. The magic went from his slippers at dawn,

and he was able to go into the house. Collie awoke and looked at him, expecting him to be very angry.

But Mr Snoot wasn't. He was strangely humble. He spoke to Collie.

'I didn't know how cold it was out there without enough straw. I didn't know how the wind blew into your kennel. I didn't see that your water was frozen. I beg your pardon. Forgive me. I have had a most dreadful night, the kind of night you must often have had. Poor Collie!'

Collie licked Mr Snoot's hand. And that day Mr Snoot filled the kennel with warm straw and swung it right away from the wind. He put fresh water down and a big dish of biscuits and bones. He didn't put Collie on the chain again.

Collie spoke to the brownie gratefully when he next saw him. 'Thank you!' he said. 'I'm very happy now – and all because I did that very big sneeze one night and blew you off your feet!'

# Stamp-About's Spell

ONE day Mr Stamp-About went through Dimity Wood in a great rage. He stamped as he went, and muttered to himself, and he even shook his fist in the air.

'I'll pay old Snorty out for not giving me what he owes me! How am I to pay my bills if he doesn't pay his? How dare he say that the apples I sold him were bad, and not worth a penny? How dare he not pay me for them?'

The rabbits fled away from his stamping feet, and the squirrels bounded up into the trees. The robin followed him, flying from tree to tree in wonder. *Now what was the matter with noisy old Stamp-About?*

Stamp-About didn't notice that he had taken the wrong path in the wood. He went on and on, and then suddenly found that the path was getting very narrow. He stopped and looked around.

'I've taken the wrong path! All because of Snorty! I am so angry with him that I don't even see the way I am walking!'

He stood there a few moments, wondering what to do.

*Perhaps there's someone nearby who will hear me if I shout, and tell me the right path*, he thought. So he gave a loud shout. 'Ho there! I want help!' Nobody answered at all, and the birds all flew away in fright, for Stamp-About had such a tremendous voice! He yelled again.

'I said, "Ho there! I want help!"'

And this time a voice called back to him – a very cross voice indeed.

'Will you be quiet? You're spoiling my spell!'

Stamp-About couldn't believe his ears. Spoiling someone's spell? Whose? And if the someone was near enough to shout back, why didn't he come to Stamp-About's help? *Rude fellow!* thought Stamp-About angrily. *I'll go and tell him what I think of him!*

So he pushed his way fiercely through the bushes, and came upon a little clearing, set neatly round with spotted red toadstools in a ring. In the middle sat a little fellow in a long black cloak that shimmered like moonlight. He had two long feelers on his forehead, the same shape as a butterfly's.

In front of him a small fire burnt, and on it was a bowl of clear glass that, strangely enough, seemed not to mind the flames at all.

'Why didn't you come to my help?' stormed Stamp-About.

'For goodness' sake go away,' said the little fellow, turning round. 'Yelling like that in my spell time! I never heard of such a thing. Go and buy yourself a few manners!'

112

Stamp-About almost exploded with temper. 'How dare you!' he cried. 'Who are you, you – you miserable, uncivil little fellow?'

'I'm Weeny, the little wizard,' said the small man. 'And I get my living by making spells at this time each day and selling them. And then you come blustering along and spoil them all. Just when I was making gold too! Pah!'

'*Gold?*' said Stamp-About in quite a different voice. 'Good gracious – can you make gold?'

'Not exactly,' said the little wizard. 'But my spells can. I've only to pop the right things into my little glass bowl here, and spell each one as they dissolve – and at the end, what do I find? A handful of gold at the bottom of my bowl!'

'Really?' said Stamp-About, wishing he hadn't been rude. 'Er, I'm sorry I disturbed you. Pray start all over again! But why do you have to spell each word – why can't you just say it?'

'Don't be silly,' said the little wizard. 'A spell is a spell because it's *spelled*, isn't it? You can't make a spell unless you spell it, can you?'

'I don't know,' said Stamp-About, and came into the toadstool ring, treading on one as he did so.

'Get out!' said the wizard, pointing a long thin finger at him. 'Treading on my magic toadstool! Get out! I'll turn you into a worm and call down that robin over there if you're not careful!'

Stamp-About hurriedly stepped out of the ring of toadstools, being very careful not to break one again. 'Now go away, and let me start my gold spell all over again,' commanded the fierce little fellow. Stamp-About tiptoed away and hid behind a tree. All right – let the wizard order him about all he liked – he would hide and watch the spell and then he would make it too when he got home! Aha – gold for the making – what a wonderful thing!

He peeped from behind a tree and watched. The wizard took no more notice of him. He had a pile of things to put into the glass bowl – but first he poured into it some water from a little jug.

Then he took up a buttercup and shredded its golden petals one by one into the bowl, muttering as he did so. Stamp-About strained his ears, but he couldn't catch what was being said, until he heard the wizard say, 'C-U-P.'

*Of course – he's only spelling the name of the flower,* thought Stamp-About. *Now, what's he putting in this time? Oh, one of the red toadstools. And now he's spelling that. Ho, what an easy spell to make!*

He watched carefully. The little wizard took another buttercup and spelled out its name – then he took a twig of hawthorn blossom and shook the white petals into the bowl, and then another buttercup.

*He's spelling everything,* thought Stamp-About. *Well, who would have thought that spelling had anything to do with the making of spells? This is going to be very useful to me! Now what's he taking?*

The wizard had now picked up the empty shell of a robin's egg, and had crushed it up and dropped it into the bubbling water, which was now changing to all colours. He muttered as he spelled the name, and then threw in yet another shower of buttercup petals.

Then he danced lightly round the bowl three times and stopped. To Stamp-About's astonishment, all the water in the bowl rose up as a cloud of steam – and there, left at the bottom, was a gleaming handful of gold!

'Look at that!' whispered Stamp-About to himself in glee, as he watched the wizard put the gold into a wallet. 'Now I know exactly how to make the spell. I'll go home and do it.'

The little wizard took up the bowl, put it into a small bag, and then he stamped out the fire. He disappeared like a shadow through the trees.

*I'll follow him*, thought Stamp-About. *He must know the way out of this wood.*

So he followed carefully, and soon came to a path he knew. He went one way and the little wizard went the other. Stamp-About was so excited that he went home smiling all over his face – much to the surprise of Snorty, who was leaning over his gate as Stamp-About passed.

'Ho! You're in a better temper now, are you?' called Snorty. 'Well, perhaps now you'll admit that those apples of yours were bad – and that I don't owe you for them after all!'

'I don't need a penny from you, Snorty, not a penny!' said Stamp-About. 'I shall soon be rich. I shall pay all the bills I haven't paid – and you'll come borrowing from me, you see if you don't!'

Well, this was very astonishing news to Snorty, who soon spread it about that Stamp-About was going to be rich. 'How?' said his friends. 'What's he going to do? Let's go round and ask him.'

When they came to Stamp-About's house he was out in his garden. He had made a small fire in the middle of the lawn, and on it he had placed a little glass bowl – the one in which his goldfish once used to swim.

'Look at that!' said Snorty in amazement. 'What's he doing? See, he's got a pile of strange things beside him – buttercups, a red toadstool and – what's that, the shell of an egg? And look, there's a spray of hawthorn blossom too, off the may hedge.'

Stamp-About saw everyone watching and was very pleased to show off. He did exactly as he had seen the little wizard do – first he threw in the buttercup petals, shredding them off the flower head one by one. As he did so, he spelled the name out loud in a high chanting voice. 'B-U-T-E-R-C-U-P!'

Then he took up the red toadstool and put that into the bowl of water too. Again he chanted out loud, spelling the name clearly. 'R-E-D-T-O-D-E-S-T-O-O-L!'

Then he shredded buttercup petals again and spelled the name as before, and then took the hawthorn blossom.

'H-O-R-T-H-O-R-N!'

And in went the white may petals as he shook the twig over the bowl! Aha – the water was changing to all kinds of colours now. Soon the handful of gold would be there!

In went more buttercup petals and the name was spelled. 'B-U-T-E-R-C-U-P!' Then he picked up the broken shell of a robin's egg.

As he crumpled up the shell and it fell into the water, Stamp-About spelled out the name in a loud voice. 'R-O-B-B-I-N-S-E-G-G!'

And last of all, another shower of golden buttercup petals went into the bubbling water. Eagerly, Stamp-About leant over it. Now for the gold! First the water would disappear in a cloud of steam, and then he would see the handful of gold at the bottom. But wait, first he must dance three times round the bowl.

Everyone crept forward to see what was about to happen. A cloud of steam shot high into the air and the water in the bowl disappeared. Then the bowl itself exploded with such a bang that everyone fell over backwards. Stamp-About sat down very suddenly indeed, scared almost out of his wits.

Then he looked eagerly at the fire. Where was the gold? Had it been scattered about all round it?

No – there wasn't a single piece of gold. The fire had gone out when the bowl exploded and now only one thing lay there – a large book!

'What's happened?' shouted Stamp-About in a rage. 'The spell's gone wrong! It should have made gold, not a stupid book. What book is it?'

He picked it up and opened it. Then he looked up

in astonishment and everyone crowded round to see what it was.

'It's a dictionary!' said Snorty and gave a huge guffaw. 'Ha, ha, ho, ho – I'm not surprised.'

'But why did the spell go wrong?' cried Stamp-About, and dashed the book to the ground. 'I don't want a dictionary!'

'Yes, you do!' chuckled Snorty. 'The spell went wrong because your spelling went wrong! Spells have to be spelled correctly! That's why all you've got is a dictionary – to help you to spell. Oh, ho, ho, ho, ho – what a joke! Can you spell rotten apples, Stamp-About? Oh, what a comical thing! He tried to make a spell – but he couldn't even spell!'

It was quite true. The spell wouldn't work unless everything was spelled out correctly, and Stamp-About had conjured up something he needed as much as gold – a dictionary. Poor old Stamp-About – he hasn't paid his bills yet!

# Woodland Wonders

# THE ENCHANTED DOLL

ANNA had a pretty doll called Victoria whom she loved very much indeed. The only thing she wished was that Victoria could walk and talk, instead of just lying or sitting perfectly still, staring at Anna with her wide-open blue eyes.

'I can pretend you talk to me, and I can pretend you run about and play,' said Anna. 'But you don't really and truly – and it *would* be such fun if just for once you would really come alive!'

Anna felt quite certain that if only Victoria *could* walk and talk, she would make her a wonderful friend, for Anna had no brothers or sisters, so she was often lonely. That was why she played so much with Victoria. But Victoria just sat and stared, and didn't move a finger or say a word!

Then one day a very strange thing happened when Anna took Victoria for a walk in Pixie Wood. Although it had such a lovely name, Anna had never seen any pixies or anything at all exciting in Pixie Wood. It was just like an ordinary wood.

But today it seemed a little different. The trees seemed closer together, as if they were nodding and whispering to one another. The sun couldn't get in between the branches, and the wood was dark and rather mysterious. Anna took Victoria by the hand and walked her over the grass, talking to her. Her doll's pram was broken and had gone to be mended, which was why Victoria was not riding in it as usual.

Anna walked on through the wood and then stopped suddenly in surprise. In front of her stood a tiny pram, a little smaller than a doll's pram, and it shone like pure gold. It had a little white hood with a silver fringe, and the pram cover was white too, with gold embroidery on it.

'Whatever is a doll's pram doing here?' wondered Anna, for she knew there were no other children about.

Anna went over to the pram and turned back the cover. There was no doll inside – but would you believe it, there was a little bottle full of milk!

'But this pram can't belong to a *real* baby!' cried Anna in astonishment. 'It's far too small. Oh! Goodness me! It might belong to a pixie baby!'

Anna waited for a little while to see if anyone came, but nobody did. Then she began to wonder. Would it matter if she wheeled Victoria about in the pram for five minutes? Surely it would do no harm. So Anna picked up her doll and strapped her in. She set the soft pillow up behind her so that she could sit up comfortably and tucked the white cover round her legs.

But as she was about to wheel her around the little wood, Anna thought she saw a little pointed

face peeping at her from behind a tree.

'Who's there?' she called. There was no answer – so Anna left the pram and ran to the tree to see if there really was a pixie peeping there. But there was no one at all except a scurrying rabbit with a white bobtail!

Anna turned back and was amazed to see the pram running away! It was wheeling off all by itself, between the trees, as fast as ever it could!

'Come back, come back!' shouted Anna. 'Oh, please, pram, do come back! Don't take Victoria away!' She ran after the pram as fast as she could, shouting as she went. The pram went faster and faster. It turned a corner by some thick bushes, and disappeared from sight.

Anna ran wildly about, and began to cry when she could not see the pram anywhere.

'Where have you gone, Victoria?' she shouted.

But there was no answer. Victoria had disappeared with the pram. Anna sat down and cried bitterly.

Presently she felt a little hand on her shoulder and a high, twittering voice said, 'What's the matter?

Would you mind getting up? You are sitting on my front door.'

Anna looked up in surprise. A tiny creature with long pointed wings, pointed ears and pointed shoes stood beside her.

'Are you a pixie?' asked Anna in astonishment. 'Am I really sitting on your front door? I'm so sorry.' She got up, and saw that she was sitting on a small yellow trapdoor, half hidden by fallen leaves.

'Why are you crying?' the pixie asked.

Anna told him all about the little pram she had found, and how it had run off with her doll.

'Oh, that pram belongs to Mother Dimity, the Old Woman Who Lives In A Shoe,' said the pixie. 'She is very forgetful, you know, and leaves it about everywhere! If she goes home without it, all she has to do is whistle for it and it will run home on its own.'

'Well, it's taken my doll too,' said Anna, beginning to cry again.

'Please don't do that,' said the pixie. 'You are making my home all damp. Anyway, you can easily

find your doll. Mother Dimity will give her back if you ask her nicely.'

'But where does she live?' asked Anna.

'Why, in the shoe of course,' said the pixie. 'Knock at the Big Oak Tree six times, go down the steps and find a boat to take you on the Underground River. Then ask the Wizard Who Grows Toadstools where the shoe is. He is sure to know, because the old woman is his sister.'

'Thank you,' said Anna, getting up. The pixie said goodbye and shut his trapdoor with a bang, leaving Anna to look for the Big Oak Tree.

Anna soon found a large oak tree. She knocked on it, but nothing happened. Then she saw the biggest oak tree she had ever seen in her life!

*That's the one!* thought Anna, and she ran over to it. She knocked on the trunk sharply six times – *rat-tat-tat-tat-tat-tat*! Then there came a creaking noise, and to her delight a small door swung open in the tree. A narrow flight of steps led downwards through the roots.

Anna slipped through the door, which at once

shut with a bang, and began to go down the steps. It was rather dark, but small lanterns hung here and there giving a little light. Anna climbed down a long way.

Eventually she came to a wide passage with a row of doors on each side. She looked closely at them. Each door had a name on it, or a message, written on a little white card.

The first card said: 'Please ring, don't knock.' The second said: 'Please knock, don't ring.' And the third door had a card that said: 'Please don't knock or ring.' As if that wasn't enough, the fourth door said: 'I am not at home yesterday or tomorrow.'

Anna thought that was very strange, and she giggled. The doors also had names on them and they were strange too.

'Mr Woozle' was on one card, and 'Dame High-Come-Quick' was on another. Anna decided to walk straight on, and at last she heard the sound of lapping water.

*That must be the Underground River*, she thought, pleased. *Now I must find a boat!*

She soon came to the riverbank. It was hung with fairy lights of all colours and looked very pretty. There were plenty of boats on the side of it, but none of them had oars. Anna looked about for someone to row her down the river, but she could see no one.

'Is there anyone here?' she shouted. Then a furry head came poking out of a funny little ticket office that Anna had not noticed.

'Yes, I'm here, and you're here too,' said the voice from the ticket office. Anna went up and saw a grey rabbit with a collar round its neck, and a spotty tie, very neatly knotted.

'Good morning,' said Anna. 'I would like to borrow a boat.'

'Here's your ticket then,' said the friendly rabbit, handing her a very chewed-looking piece of cardboard.

'How much is it?' asked Anna.

'Oh, nothing!' he replied cheerily. 'Everything is free here!'

'Where's the boatman?' asked Anna.

'Nowhere,' said the rabbit. 'There isn't one.'

'Then how can I go anywhere?' asked Anna.

'Climb in,' said the rabbit, 'and the boat will take you.'

Anna frowned at the rabbit, and walked up to one of the boats. She chose a blue one dotted with gold stars, and climbed into it. At once the boat set off by itself.

It shot on down the river, and after a little while it left the underground tunnel and came out into the open air. The boat sped on and on, and Anna saw with surprise that the surrounding fields were full of animals dressed up like human beings.

Suddenly Anna saw a curious sight. In the middle of a field stood a strange-looking old man waving a stick about. He was surrounded by toadstools of all sizes, colours and shapes, and she guessed that he must be the Wizard Who Grows Toadstools.

'Stop, stop!' she cried to the boat. It stopped at once and headed towards the bank. Anna patted the boat, said thank you and then jumped out. She went up to the old wizard. He didn't see her at first and almost knocked her over with his silver wand.

'Please,' she said. 'I've come to ask you where your sister, the Old Woman Who Lives In A Shoe, is. I want to go and speak to her.'

'You'll find her on the other side of that hill,' said the wizard, waving his wand violently. 'Look out! You are standing just where my next toadstool is growing!'

Just then Anna felt the earth pushing up under her feet. A big toadstool appeared right beneath her. It was covered with big red spots.

'Thank you,' said Anna, and ran out of the field as quickly as she could. She made her way to the hill in the distance. She climbed it, and as soon as she came to the top she saw the shoe.

It was enormous, and it had windows and doors and a chimney at the top. Anna thought it looked lovely. She ran down to it, and at once she was surrounded by a crowd of small pixie children with pointed faces, pointed ears and short wings.

'Who are you? Where do you come from?' they cried in excitement. 'Have you come to see our new child?'

'You can see her through the window!' said a tiny pixie, taking Anna's hand and leading her to a window. Anna peeped in – and there, in the bed nearest the window, lay Victoria, her very own doll!

'She arrived today in Mother Dimity's pram,' explained the pixie. 'But she won't talk, or eat or drink. She won't even blink her eyes!'

'That's because she isn't a little girl at all,' cried Anna. 'She's my doll and her name is Victoria!'

'A doll!' said the pixie children, crowding round Anna. 'What's a doll? We don't know what a doll is.'

'Well, a doll is – a doll is – well, that's what a doll is!' said Anna, pointing to where Victoria lay on the little bed.

'But can't the poor thing move or talk at all?' asked the pixies in surprise.

'Of course not,' said Anna and she ran in through the door of the big shoe, and bumped into the old woman.

'Now then, gently, gently!' said Mother Dimity. 'You'll frighten the new little girl, rushing about like that. I've just given her some very strong magic

medicine to make her come alive again.'

'She never has been alive!' cried Anna. 'She's my doll!'

'Your doll!' said the old woman. 'Oh goodness! I remember once seeing a doll in the Land of Boys and Girls. Well, she looks a lot like a little girl, don't you agree? And she'll be even more like one now that I've given her the medicine.'

'Do you mean to say that Victoria will be able to walk and talk?' cried Anna.

'Of course,' said Mother Dimity. 'Look – she is blinking her eyes now! Perhaps I had better change her back into a doll again.'

'No, please don't,' said Anna at once. She ran to Victoria and looked at her. The little doll was opening and shutting her eyes and she suddenly looked at Anna and smiled a wide smile, showing all her pretty teeth.

'Hallo,' she said. 'I've often wanted to talk to you, and now I can!'

'Oh, what fun we'll have together now!' Anna cried, hugging her doll to her. 'We can talk to one another, and play all kinds of games.'

'But you mustn't let anyone but yourself know,' said Mother Dimity at once. 'If you do, the magic will disappear, and Victoria will be an ordinary doll again.'

'Oh, I won't tell anyone at all!' said Anna happily. 'Come on, Victoria, we'll go home now. It must be getting late.'

Mother Dimity showed them a quick way home, and they arrived there just in time for dinner. Anna put Victoria in her cot, and told her to be sure not to move if anyone came in, and she promised. And now Anna is as happy as can be, for she has a real live doll to play with her, and they *do* have some fine games together.

'Really!' Anna's mother often says. 'You might think that doll was alive, the way Anna plays with her all day long!'

And then Anna smiles a big smile – but she doesn't say a word! She has a wonderful secret to keep and she keeps it very well!

# A Basket of Surprises

WHEN Jimmy's mother went to the garden fair at the vicarage she bought a very beautiful basket. It was large and round and deep, and had a fine, strong handle. All round the basket was a pretty green and yellow pattern. It really was a very fine basket, and Jimmy's mother was pleased with it.

'Now, you are not to borrow this basket for anything, Jimmy,' she said to him. 'You can have my old one, if you want one. This is to be kept for special things, like taking eggs to Granny, or something like that.'

Jimmy promised. He was once allowed to take some flowers in the basket to old Mr White, but that was all. And then one day he wanted a basket to take his trains, signals and lines to the house of his friend, Billy Brown. He went to find the old basket and it wasn't there. His mother was out and no one was at home except Tibby, the big tabby cat, sitting by the fire.

'Where's the old basket, Tibby?' Jimmy asked her. But she just mewed and stayed sitting by the fire, thinking her pussy thoughts. Jimmy hunted everywhere. There was no old basket to be found at all. Perhaps his mother had taken it.

'Well, I'll have to take the new basket,' said Jimmy. 'I can't possibly take all my things without a basket.'

So he took down the beautiful new basket and packed his things into it. Then off he went to Billy's and had a fine tea and a fine game. Billy begged him to lend him his railway for a day, so Jimmy said he

would. He set off home with the empty basket, swinging it by the big handle.

He had to go through the woods on his way home, and as he ran he saw a bird fly into a bush. *Hallo!* thought Jimmy. *There's a nest there. I'll just peep and see. I won't disturb the bird in case it deserts its nest – but I would just like to see if there are any baby birds there.*

He pushed his way into the bush, but the bird flew out again and into another bush. Jimmy followed her. He felt sure she must have a nest somewhere. But she hadn't. She was just looking for the caterpillars there.

Jimmy set off home again – but suddenly he remembered that he had put down his basket somewhere. Goodness! Where could it be?

He ran back – but no matter how he looked he couldn't find that basket anywhere! *Oh dear!* thought Jimmy, as he hunted. *Whatever will Mummy say if I go home without it? I am sure I put it down by the bush I first looked in.*

But Jimmy couldn't find the bush! And at last he

had to go home without the basket. When he told his mother he had lost it she was very cross.

'You are a naughty boy, Jimmy,' she said. 'I told you not to borrow my best basket. Now, unless it is found again, you must save up your money and buy me a new one.'

'Oh, but, Mummy, I'm saving up to buy a railway tunnel!' cried Jimmy in dismay.

'Well, I'm sorry, dear, but you can't buy your tunnel until you have bought a new basket,' said his mother. 'You had better go and have another hunt for it.'

Poor Jimmy! He went and hunted and hunted, but he could not find that basket! The next day his Uncle Peter came to see him and gave him some money to spend – but his mother said he was to put it all into his moneybox to save up for the new basket. He was dreadfully disappointed. The next morning his mother called him and said, 'Have you seen Tibby, Jimmy? She isn't in her usual place by the fire, and she hasn't been in for her breakfast.'

'No, I haven't seen her,' said Jimmy, quite worried,

for he was very fond of Tibby. 'Where can she be?'

'Perhaps she will come in for her dinner,' said his mother. But Tibby didn't. There was no sign of her at all. Jimmy got more and more worried. He had had Tibby from a kitten, and the two were great friends. He did so hope she hadn't got caught in a trap.

'Do you think she has, Mummy?' he asked. 'Oh, wouldn't it be dreadful if she had gone rabbiting in the woods and got caught in a trap and nobody was there to set her free?'

'Oh, I don't expect she has, for a moment,' said his mother. 'She hardly ever goes rabbiting. She will turn up, I expect. Now, what are you going to do this afternoon, Jimmy? You said you wanted to go and play with Billy Brown.'

'Well, I did want to,' said Jimmy. 'But I think I'll just go and hunt for Tibby, Mummy. I do feel unhappy about her, really I do.'

'After tea we will catch the bus and go into the town to buy a new basket,' said his mother. 'I really must have another. I think you have enough money in your box now to buy me one.'

Jimmy went off to hunt for Tibby, feeling very miserable. 'I've lost Tibby, and I've got to give up my railway tunnel and buy a new basket instead,' he sighed, as he ran along to the woods. 'What a lot of bad luck all at once!'

He soon came to the woods, and he began hunting about, calling Tibby. He felt sure she must have been caught in a trap.

'Tibby, Tibby, Tibby!' he cried. 'Where are you? Tibby, Tibby, Tibby!'

For some time he could hear nothing but the wind in the trees and the singing of the birds. Then he thought he heard a small mew.

'Tibby!' he shouted. 'Tibby!'

'Miaow!' said a pussy voice, and up ran Tibby to Jimmy, and purred and rubbed herself against his legs.

'Oh, dear Tibby!' said Jimmy, really delighted to see his cat again. He picked her up in his arms and made a fuss of her. She purred loudly, and then tried to get down.

145

'No, I'll carry you home, Tibby,' said Jimmy, and he turned to go home. But Tibby struggled very hard, and at last he had to let her go. She ran into the woods and disappeared. Jimmy was very much puzzled. He went after her.

'Tibby! Why don't you want to come home with me?' he called. 'Come back! Where are you going?'

Tibby mewed from somewhere; then Jimmy saw her bright green eyes looking at him from a nearby bush! He ran up and knelt down to see where she was.

And will you believe it, Tibby was lying comfortably down in the fine new basket that Jimmy had lost when he was looking for the bird's nest! There she was, as cosy as anything, looking up at Jimmy.

But there was still another surprise for the little boy, for when Tibby jumped out of the basket, what do you suppose he saw at the bottom? Why, five beautiful little tabby kittens, all exactly like Tibby! He stared and stared and stared! He simply couldn't believe his eyes!

'Oh, Tibby!' he said. 'Oh, Tibby! I've found you – and the basket – and some kittens too! Oh, whatever will Mummy say?'

He picked up the basket with the kittens and set off home. Tibby ran beside him mewing. When he got home he called his mother and showed her his surprising find.

She was just as astonished as he was! 'Oh, Tibby,

what darling little kittens!' she cried. 'You shall have them in your own cosy basket by the fire! Fancy you finding our basket in the woods and putting your kittens there!'

'Mummy, I needn't spend my money on a new basket now, need I?' said Jimmy, pleased. 'I can buy my tunnel with my money.'

'Of course!' said his mother. 'We will just put Tibby comfortably in her own basket with the kittens, and then we will catch the bus and go and buy your tunnel. You deserve it, really, Jimmy, because you gave up your afternoon's play with Billy to go and hunt for Tibby – and you found a basket of surprises, didn't you?'

So everyone was happy, and Jimmy got his railway tunnel after all. As for Tibby, she was very happy to be made such a fuss of, and you should have seen her kittens when they grew! They were the prettiest, dearest little things you could wish to see. I know, because, you see, I've got one of them for my own!

# THE TALE OF BUSHY THE FOX

**B**USHY was a young fox. He lived with his father and mother and little brothers and sisters in a den under a big gorse bush on the common. But he wasn't at all happy there.

He wanted to go out and explore the world, but his mother wouldn't let him.

'Why can't I?' said Bushy crossly. 'The rabbits play over there on the hillside, and nobody tells them not to. The horse and the donkey are down there in

the field and come to no harm. The dog barks down at the farmyard and I see him wandering about all over the place. Why can't I go where I like? I am as clever as anybody else.'

'Oh, no you're not!' said his mother sharply. 'It's only stupid foxes that want to leave their den before they are old enough. You must learn all kinds of things from me and your father before you are allowed out alone. You may be chased by hounds – what would you do then? You may find a farmer with a gun, and he will shoot you – what would you do then?'

'Oh, I daresay I should think of something,' said the fox cub. 'Anyway, I don't want to grow up to be a fox, if I'm going to be hunted like that. I'd rather be a dog, or a cat, or a horse or even a hen! Men keep all those things and feed them well; I don't want to be a fox.'

'Well, let me tell you this – you couldn't do any of the things that those creatures are clever enough to do,' said his mother, cuffing him. 'You think you are clever, don't you, Master Bushy? – but you're not!'

Bushy was angry when his mother cuffed him. He went right to the back of the den and thought and thought.

*When nobody is looking tonight, I will slip out of the hole*, he thought. *I will visit the dog and the cat, the horse and the hen, and I will see if I can grow up into something else instead of a fox!*

So that night, when his father and mother were out hunting for food, and his brothers and sisters lay all curled up in a heap, fast asleep, Bushy crept out of the den. He scampered down the hillside to the farm.

The first creature he saw was old Captain, the brown-and-white horse. He was standing under a tree, half asleep. Bushy made him jump when he spoke to him.

'Excuse me, big horse, but will you please tell me if it's easy to be a horse?' asked Bushy politely.

Captain tried to see who was talking to him, but he couldn't.

'Oh, it's quite easy,' he said. 'You have to be able to do a few things, of course.'

'What do you have to do?' asked Bushy.

'Oh, nothing much,' said Captain. 'You must be able to pull a cart, to plough a field, to carry a rider. You must wear a saddle and bridle, you must know which way to go when your master twitches the reins, you must—'

'Oh dear!' said Bushy in dismay. 'I should never be able to do all that! Good evening to you. I shan't be a horse.'

The next creature he saw was the cat, Mouser. She was lying down on a mat outside the farmhouse door. She couldn't see Bushy, but she answered him when he spoke.

'Excuse me, cat, but will you please tell me if it's easy to be a cat?' asked Bushy.

'Oh, it's quite easy,' said Mouser. 'You have to be able to do a few things, of course.'

'What do you have to do?' asked Bushy.

'Oh, nothing much,' said Mouser. 'You must be able to catch all the mice, and fight the rats – and they can bite very fiercely! You must be able to mew when you are hungry, and purr when you are pleased. You must—'

'Oh my!' said Bushy. 'I could never mew or purr, I know! And I'm afraid of rats, just at present. Good evening to you. I shan't be a cat!'

He went on his way once more, and soon came to the henhouse. One hen was awake, and Bushy spoke to her through the wire netting. She couldn't see him, or she might have been frightened.

'Excuse me, hen, but will you please tell me if it's easy to be a hen?' he asked politely.

'Oh, it's quite easy,' said the hen. 'You have to be able to lay eggs, of course, and cackle loudly when you've laid them. You have to be able to bring up chicks, and cluck, and you must always obey the cockerel.'

'Well, I could never obey a silly old cockerel!' said Bushy. 'And I couldn't ever lay an egg, I'm sure. Good evening to you. I shan't be a hen!'

Very soon he came to where a large pig lay in a sty.

'Excuse me, pig,' said Bushy, 'but will you please tell me if it's easy to be a pig?'

'Very easy,' said the pig, grunting, 'and it's easier still to be bacon! I'll change places with you, if you like. You can live a lazy life here in my sty and be made into bacon in the autumn, and I'll run about free and live my life in the open!'

'Oh my, I never want to be bacon!' said the fox cub, shivering. 'Good evening to you. I shan't be a pig!'

Off he went again, and came to the dog's kennel. Pincher, the sheepdog, was wide awake, and he sniffed at Bushy as he came near.

'Excuse me, dog, but will you please tell me if it's easy to be a dog?' Bushy asked politely.

'Oh, it's quite easy,' said Pincher. 'You have to be able to do a few things, of course.'

'What do you have to do?' asked Bushy.

'Well, you must be able to look after sheep, and see that those clever foxes don't take the lambs,' said Pincher. 'You must be able to guard the farmyard and see that no fox steals the hens. You must look after the young ducks, for those sly foxes are always after them. You must be able to bark at foxes, and seize them – like this!'

Pincher suddenly leapt at Bushy, and very nearly caught him. The frightened cub jumped away just in time. Pincher began to snarl and growl.

'I know you're a fox!' he snapped. 'What do you mean by coming into my farmyard and asking foolish questions? Whoever heard of a fox wanting to be any other animal! Why, foxes are the cleverest creatures in the countryside! Wuff! Wuff-wuff!'

Pincher began to bark loudly, and the farmer threw up his window and leant out. The ducks quacked, the hens clucked, the pig grunted. What a fearful noise there was!

Bushy was glad to slink out of the farmyard unseen. He raced back to his den on the hillside and was very happy to be curled up among his brothers and sisters once more.

*How foolish I am to want to be some other creature, not a fox*, he thought. *Why, no other animal is so clever! Who wants to drag a plough, to lay an egg, to mew and purr, or to look after hens and ducks? No, I will catch hens and ducks, I will make that barking dog afraid of me. I want to be a fox and nothing else!*

How surprised Bushy's mother was next day to find what an obedient little cub Bushy was. She didn't know he had been out all night, talking to the farmyard creatures – and Bushy didn't tell her, because he knew she would cuff him!

# THE TALE OF JIG AND JOG

ONE day Jig and Jog, the two brownies who lived in Hollyhock Cottage, made up their minds to give a party.

'We shall say it's a birthday party,' said Jig. 'Then everyone will bring us presents. Won't that be nice, Jog?'

'Rather!' said Jog, rubbing his horny little hands in glee. 'Ha! Presents of cakes! And sweets! And all kinds of exciting things!'

157

'We will give our party on November the fourteenth,' said Jig. 'We will send out the invitation cards now.'

'Who shall come to the party?' said Jog.

'Well, we will ask Prickles the hedgehog,' said Jig. 'He makes beautiful cakes. He might bring us one. We will put on our invitation cards that it is a birthday party. Then he will know he must bring a present.'

'Who else shall come?' asked Jog.

'Well, Slinky the snake would be a good person to ask,' said Jig, 'and so would Slow-One the toad; and his cousin, Hoppity the frog. Oh, and don't you think we could ask that bird who plays hide-and-seek so well – what's his name now?'

'You mean the cuckoo,' said Jog. 'Yes, we will ask him too; and we will ask Dozy the little dormouse, for he is a generous fellow, and might even bring us a present each, instead of one between us.'

The two brownies made out their list and then wrote out their invitation cards.

*Please come to a birthday party at
Hollyhock Cottage on November
the fourteenth, at four o'clock.*

Then they posted all the cards in the pillar box at the
end of the road, and waited for the answers.

The postman, Floppy the rabbit, took the cards
and went to deliver them. He knew where Prickles
the hedgehog lived: in a cosy hole in the sunny
bankside of the hedge. He slipped the card into the
hole. He knew where Slinky the snake lived too – in
the old hollow tree in the middle of the wood. He
climbed up and dropped the card down into the
hole. He was a very good postman.

Then Floppy took Slow-One's card, and went to
a big stone by the pond. He knew Slow-One the toad
lived there. He pushed the card under the stone and
left it. Hoppity the frog lived in the pond. Floppy
waited until a stickleback came up to the top of the
water and asked him to take the card to Hoppity.
The fish caught the card neatly in its mouth and
swam off with it.

159

'Now there's the card for the cuckoo,' said Floppy Rabbit to himself. 'Well, he was always sitting in that big beech tree, calling cuckoo to everyone, so I'll put his card there. He is sure to see it if he sits there again.'

Floppy had only one card left now – and that was for Dozy the dormouse. Floppy knew quite well where Dozy was living. He was in a cosy hole deep down in the roots of the big fir tree at the edge of the wood, not far from Floppy's own burrow. So, being a sensible rabbit, Floppy left that card till last, stuffed it into Dozy's hole, and then slipped into his own burrow for a rest and a cup of carrot tea.

Jig and Jog waited impatiently for the answers to their invitations. But none came! It was most extraordinary. Jig and Jog were puzzled. And then Jig thought he knew why. They had not put on the cards that they wanted an answer! So perhaps all their guests had thought they need not reply. Well, it didn't matter. The two brownies felt quite sure they would all turn up at the party on the right day – each bringing a very nice present!

They began to get ready for the party. They each had a new suit made, a red one for Jig and a blue one for Jog. They made a batch of chocolate cakes and a batch of ginger ones. They made strawberry-jam sandwiches. They put out a clean cloth and arranged chairs all round their small table.

'We said four o'clock on the invitation cards,' said Jig, when the day came. 'It's half past three now. Are we quite, quite ready, Jog?'

'Well, we've put on our new suits, and we've laid the table and put out the cakes and sandwiches and arranged the chairs,' said Jog. 'Yes, we are quite ready. I wonder who will come first!'

'And I wonder what everyone will bring us,' said Jig. 'It's a good thing we told everyone it was a birthday party, so that we can get presents.'

Four o'clock came – but nobody walked up the garden path. How strange! Quarter past four and still no guests! Half past four – five o'clock! Where could everyone be? There were the cakes and the sandwiches – but no guests to eat them. Jig and Jog looked as if they were going to cry!

They went down the garden path and looked up and down the road. Only Dame Chippy was there, coming along with the washing. When she saw their sad faces she stopped.

'What's the matter?' she asked.

'Well,' said Jig mournfully, 'we sent out invitations

to Prickles, Slinky, Slow-One, Hoppity and Cuckoo and Dozy to come to a birthday party today – and nobody's come – and we shan't get any presents.'

'Don't you know that you never tell anyone a party is a *birthday* party?' said Dame Chippy, shocked. 'Why, that's just asking for presents, and nobody with good manners does that. It serves you right that nobody has come.'

'But *why* haven't they come?' wailed Jog.

'If you think hard, you'll know,' said Dame Chippy with a grin.

Jig and Jog thought hard – but they didn't know. Do you? Dame Chippy had to tell them.

'You are two silly creatures,' she said. 'Don't you know that Prickles the hedgehog always finds a hole for himself in the winter and sleeps the cold days away? Don't you know that Slinky the snake hates the cold and hides in a hollow tree fast asleep until the spring comes? And Slow-One the toad is never awake in the winter, sillies! He is sound asleep under his big stone – and his cousin, Hoppity the frog, is hidden in the mud at the bottom of the pond!

163

As for the cuckoo, he has left the land months ago. He always goes south for the winter to find warmth and food.'

'What about Dozy?' asked Jig in a small voice.

'He sleeps more soundly than any of them!' said Dame Chippy. 'He's snoring in the roots of the old fir tree! Well, well, well – no wonder you have no guests and no birthday presents! It serves you right for being so stupid and greedy!'

'Oh, all our cards were wasted, and all our cakes will be wasted too,' wept Jig and Jog in dismay.

'Your cakes needn't be wasted!' said Dame Chippy. 'I'll come in and eat them for you!'

And so she did – Jig and Jog weren't a bit pleased. What sillies they were, weren't they?

# BINKLE'S WONDERFUL PICTURE

**B**INKLE the bunny woke up one morning and tried to remember a dream he had had. He stared up at the ceiling and thought. It had been a very nice dream – he had done something that everyone admired – now, what was it?

'I know!' he cried suddenly, banging the bedclothes. 'I painted a wonderful picture!'

'Binkle,' shouted Flip angrily, waking up with a jump, 'stop hitting me!'

'You shouldn't be so near me then,' said Binkle. 'Listen, Flip, to my wonderful dream. I dreamt I painted a marvellous picture of Oak Tree Town, and I dreamt that Rombo the famous painter-rabbit came and told me it was the best picture he had ever seen. Fancy that!'

'What was the picture like?' asked Flip, very interested.

'That's the funny part,' said Binkle, frowning. 'However much I looked at it, I couldn't seem to see any picture at all. But everybody else did.'

'Hmm – rather a silly dream,' said Flip, suddenly feeling sleepy again, and began to snore before Binkle could tell him any more.

But Binkle went on thinking about it, until, half awake and half asleep, he found himself smiling over an absurd idea that had just occurred to him. He gave a chuckle.

'I'll do it,' he said, 'and see what happens.'

He went on planning until he had everything clear in his mind. Then he woke Flip up and told him what he was going to do.

'Don't be silly, Binkle!' said Flip. 'You must be half asleep to think of a thing like that.'

'I'm very much awake, thank you,' said Binkle, and tweaked Flip's nose, so that he squealed in anger and sat up to pummel Binkle.

But Binkle was already out of bed. 'That's right, Flip,' he chuckled. 'I thought that would wake you up.'

The two rabbits dressed quickly and got their breakfast. While they were having it, Binkle told Flip what he was to do that morning, and gave him a long list of things to buy.

'And mind you tell everyone I'm going to paint a wonderful picture,' he ended.

Off went Flip to buy paintbrushes, paints, canvas, an easel and a palette. He bought them all, but wouldn't let them be wrapped up. He wanted everyone to see them.

Carrying them all carefully, he went slowly down the street, meeting Herbert Hedgehog, Dilly Duck, Derry Dormouse and Riggles Rat, and many others who were doing their morning shopping.

'Goodness gracious!' they all cried, as one by one they met him. 'What in the world are you going to do, Flip Bunny?'

'I'm just taking these home to Binkle,' Flip told everyone. 'He's got an idea for a wonderful picture. Oak Tree Town will be proud of it, I can tell you!'

'Fiddlesticks!' grunted Herbert Hedgehog. 'You can't make *me* believe Binkle can paint.'

'You don't know what Binkle can do,' answered Flip. 'You just wait and see his picture, Herbert.'

Well, of course, all Oak Tree Town was very interested in Binkle's new work. They didn't quite know what to think about it. Binkle was a surprising bunny, and nobody ever knew what he would do next.

So everybody talked about his painting and wondered how it was getting on and whether anyone would be allowed to see it. Which was just what Binkle wanted them to do.

Binkle was very busy. He had found a nice sheltered spot in the garden, and here he had put up his easel and canvas. He had also brought out his little stool and all his brushes and paints. He mixed a little of each colour on his enormous palette and thought it looked very artistic indeed.

But he didn't put a single dab of paint on his canvas. That was left quite empty.

Then he sent Flip into the woods with a spade and told him to dig up any old roots he could see, and if anyone asked him what he wanted, to say that he was taking Blue Fuzzymuz, Red Rillobies and Purple Pittitoos for Binkle to mix with his paints.

'But why?' asked Flip, most astonished.

'To make my picture magic!' answered Binkle, with a chuckle.

So off went Flip with a sack and dug up bluebell roots and violet roots.

Riggles Rat saw him doing it, and wanted to know why.

'I'm taking Blue Fuzzymuz, Red Rillobies and Purple Pittitoos to Binkle,' answered Flip. 'He mixes them with his paints, you know, and they make his picture magic.'

'How?' asked Riggles, amazed.

'I don't quite know yet,' answered Flip truthfully, going on his way with the heavy sack. 'Tell you tomorrow, p'raps.'

Riggles was most curious. 'Come to tea with me tomorrow,' he cried, 'and tell me all about it.'

'Right!' said Flip and went off.

He told Binkle about his meeting with Riggles, and Binkle laughed till he cried.

'Go and put those old roots in the shed,' he said, 'and then come back and I'll tell you what to say to him.'

When Flip came back, Binkle took him to his easel in the garden.

'What do you see there!' he asked, pointing to the empty canvas.

'Nothing,' answered Flip, rather astonished.

'Well, listen,' said Binkle solemnly. 'I'm painting a picture there that only *clever* people can see. Stupid ones won't see anything at all. It's magic, you see. My dream gave me the idea. When the picture's finished, we'll let people in to see it at a penny a time!'

Flip stared at him. He wished he hadn't said he could see nothing. Then something in Binkle's smile made him ask a question.

'Binkle,' he said, 'are you *really* painting a picture?'

'No, not really,' said Binkle. 'But I don't expect anyone will like to say so, in case we think they're stupid. We'll just see how many people we take in, Flip. But I'm going to get Rombo the painter-rabbit to say it's wonderful first.'

'Rombo! But he'd never come. And he'd say you hadn't painted a picture at all,' cried Flip.

'Not the real Rombo! I'm going to ask my cousin Rab the bunny from Bracken Hill Town to dress up and pretend he's Rombo,' chuckled Binkle. 'I've written to ask him to come on Friday. What fun! You must be sure and tell Riggles that, when you go to tea with him tomorrow.'

So next day off went Flip, dressed in his best, to see Riggles the rat. He found that Herbert Hedgehog was there too, and Mowdie Mole, all very eager to hear the latest news of Binkle's painting.

Flip, feeling thoroughly naughty, began to enjoy himself.

'Oh, yes,' he said in answer to their questions. 'Binkle's picture is getting on finely. It's a picture of Oak Tree Town and he's putting *everybody* into it!'

'Is he *really*?' said Herbert, most interested, hoping that he was somewhere well in the front of the picture. 'But isn't there supposed to be something magic about this picture, Flip?'

'Rather!' said Flip. 'He's mixed all sorts of peculiar juices in with his paints – I believe his great-grandmother once told him the secret – and – isn't this strange? – only really clever people can see the picture! Stupid people can't see a thing – it just looks like empty canvas to them!'

Nobody spoke for a minute. They were too astonished and too busy wondering whether they would be able to see this extraordinary picture or not.

Flip went boldly on.

'And Rombo the famous painter-rabbit is coming to see it on Friday,' he said. 'Fancy that!'

'Dear, dear, dear!' said Mowdie Mole, quite

breathless with surprise. 'I'd no idea Binkle could paint.'

Nobody could talk of anything else all teatime but Binkle's wonderful picture. And when Flip went home, he felt quite certain that everyone in Oak Tree Town would know about it before night had fallen. And he was quite right. They did! Mowdie, Riggles and Herbert saw to that.

Herbert was tremendously excited. He was longing to see the wonderful picture, and longing to know what Rombo said about it. He decided to go up to Binkle's cottage on Friday afternoon and see whether Rombo really had arrived. Riggles said he'd go with him, and Sammy Squirrel too.

So on Friday afternoon all three walked into Binkle's little white gate, and saw Binkle sitting in the garden.

'Good afternoon,' he said kindly. 'I'm so sorry I can't ask you to stay, but I'm expecting Flip to bring Rombo here any minute to see my picture. But do call again afterwards, if you like.'

Rather crossly the three went out again.

'Let's hide here by this tree and hear what Rombo says,' whispered Riggles.

So all three hid silently behind the oak tree that stood next to Binkle's garden. But Binkle was watching out of the corner of his eye and knew quite well they were there. He chuckled to himself.

Presently Flip came up the hill with another rabbit. He was dressed in a black velvet coat and had a long flowing tie and wore very big glasses. Behind both his big ears were stuck lots of paintbrushes.

'Oh, good afternoon, Rombo Rabbit,' said Binkle politely. 'It is very good of you to waste your time on me and my picture.'

'Not at all, not at all,' said the make-believe Rombo, who was quite enjoying his part, especially as Flip had promised him a glorious tea afterwards. 'Where is your picture?'

'Here,' said Binkle, leading the way to where his easel stood in the shelter of the bushes.

Rombo peered at it closely. Then he stepped back and looked at it. Then he gazed at it sideways, and finally he went behind it. He came out in front of it again at last, and shook Binkle warmly by the paw.

'Binkle,' he said, 'it's *wonderful*!'

Herbert, Riggles and Sammy, hidden behind the tree, looked at each other and shook with excitement.

'Did you hear that?' whispered Herbert. 'Binkle's a clever chap!'

'Sh!' said Sammy. 'Rombo's talking again.'

'In fact,' went on Rombo, 'it's *more* than wonderful – it's magic! Magic! Binkle, did you know that?'

'I hoped it might be,' said Binkle modestly.

'Yes,' said Rombo, shaking Binkle by the other paw. 'Mark my words, Binkle Bunny, no stupid person will be able to see that picture of yours. It will only be visible to clever people. Ha! Ha! Now you'll be able to see who's clever and who isn't in Oak Tree Town! Ha! Ha!'

'Ha! Ha!' said Binkle.

'Ha, ha, *ha*!' roared Flip, who had been nearly bursting all the time.

The three hidden behind the oak tree didn't laugh.

They were all wondering which of them would be clever enough to see Binkle's picture. Herbert felt *quite* sure he would.

'Better wait here till Rombo's gone,' he whispered. 'Then we'll go and see it.'

The three rascally bunnies were having a glorious tea, and chuckling over the thought of the hidden listeners by the oak tree.

'You did your part well,' said Binkle to Rab, 'but why in the world did you go behind the picture, Rab?'

'He, he! To laugh, of course!' said Rab, stuffing a whole lettuce into his mouth. 'I could see Sammy Squirrel's tail sticking out, and I nearly choked. Ha, ha!'

'Ha, ha!' went Binkle.

'Ha, ha, *ha*!' squealed Flip, who was almost ill with laughing. He never could stop, once he really began.

At last Binkle sent Flip home with Rab. Then he sauntered out into the garden, pulling his lovely whiskers and twitching his big ears. He went to the front gate. Ah! there were Herbert, Riggles and Sammy Squirrel coming along, all looking rather sheepish.

'May we see your picture now?' asked Herbert.

'Er, well, I was thinking of charging a penny to see it,' said Binkle. 'But I'll let *you* in for nothing, Herbert. The others can see it afterwards if they like to pay a penny.'

'We'll wait and see what Herbert says,' said Sammy cautiously.

So Herbert, feeling very honoured to be let in for nothing, followed Binkle to where his easel stood in the bushes.

When he got there, he stared at the canvas in the greatest dismay – for he couldn't see any picture on it at all!

*That means I'm very stupid!* he thought miserably. *Dear, dear, dear, and Oak Tree Town has always thought me so clever! I must pretend I see a picture. It must be wonderful if Rombo admired it!*

'Well, what do you think of it?' asked Binkle. 'Do you think the sky is blue enough?'

'Er, er, yes, quite!' said Herbert, pretending to look very close. 'Oh, yes, decidedly. Oh, it's a wonderful picture, Binkle – wonderful! I shouldn't have thought you could have done it!'

'Oh, it was quite easy,' said Binkle truthfully.

'Er, I'll go and tell Sammy and Riggles to come,' said Herbert, terrified that Binkle might ask him a question he couldn't answer. He hurried to the gate and beckoned to them.

'What's it like?' they asked. 'Is it worth a penny?'

'Oh, yes, yes!' said Herbert. 'It's marvellous! Wonderful! Extraordinary! You really must come and see it! It's got a lovely blue sky!'

Well, Sammy and Riggles each paid Binkle a penny and went in. They couldn't believe their eyes when they saw an empty canvas!

*To think old Herbert's clever enough to see it, and I'm not!* thought Sammy Squirrel in great disgust. *I'm not going to say I can't see it, anyway.*

And Riggles thought just the same, and they began to praise it mightily.

'Finest picture I ever saw,' said Riggles, 'and the blue sky is lovely.'

'Yes, I'm rather pleased with that myself,' said Binkle. 'What do you think of the picture, Sammy?'

Well, Sammy thought a whole lot of things, but he wasn't going to say them. He asked a question.

'Who's that on the left-hand side of the picture?' he asked, pretending to look at it very hard.

'That!' said Binkle in a tone of great surprise. 'Why, that's Herbert! Fancy you not recognising dear old Herbert!'

Herbert bristled all over with importance.

'*I* recognised myself,' he said most untruthfully, 'and it's a *very* good portrait, Binkle!'

'Oh, very!' said Riggles, wishing to goodness *he* could see it.

'Best portrait of the lot, I think,' said Binkle, 'though of course Sammy's very good too. That's him balancing a nut on his nose. Look—' and he pointed to the right-hand side of the canvas.

How Sammy wished he could see it! It made him feel quite ill, and he thought he'd better go home

before the others guessed his stupidity.

The other two said at once that they would go too, and after thanking Binkle very politely for letting them see his masterpiece, they went off down the hill, solemnly talking about Binkle's picture.

'The sky was wonderfully good,' said Herbert.

'It was wonderful,' agreed Riggles.

'But your portrait was lifelike,' said Sammy, determined to keep his end up.

Well, of course everyone in Oak Tree Town wanted to know what Rombo had said and what the picture was like. All three said it was wonderful and well worth a penny to go and see.

'Of course,' said Sammy with a laugh, 'you won't all see it, you know! Stupid people can't see a thing! It's a magic sort of picture.'

Everyone was most anxious to go and look at Binkle's picture, and next day the pennies began to pour in.

Dilly Duck came first, and could hardly believe her eyes when she saw nothing on the canvas.

*I always had a sort of feeling I was stupid, and*

*now I know it*, she thought miserably. But aloud she said, 'Yes, yes yes! A lovely picture! The blue sky is exactly the right colour.'

'Everybody says that,' said Binkle modestly. 'And do you like the trees?'

Dilly looked closely at the canvas and wished heartily she could see what the trees looked like.

'They're *very* nice,' she said, and then suddenly she said she must go home in case anyone wanted stamps. She was afraid Binkle would ask her more questions she couldn't answer. She didn't want him to guess she couldn't see anything.

Mowdie Mole, Susie Squirrel and Derry Dormouse came, but they didn't stay long. They all said the picture was marvellous, especially the blue sky, and Herbert's portrait, and then they hurried off for fear anyone would guess they were pretending.

Creeper Mouse wanted to know if he could bring his children and Bess Bunny asked if she could bring hers.

'Oh, of course,' answered Binkle, 'but it won't be

any use, you know. Children won't be clever enough yet to see my picture. But do bring them!'

So all Bess Bunny's children and Creeper Mouse's family came, and it was just as Binkle had said.

'*I* can't see any pretty picture!' said little Bobbin Bunny.

'I can't see anything!' said wee Mixie Mouse, nearly crying with disappointment.

Of course Bess Bunny and Creeper Mouse couldn't bear to be thought as stupid as their children, so they both said they *loved* the picture and thought it the best they'd ever seen.

Very soon everyone in Oak Tree Town had paid a penny to see Binkle's picture, and all of them, except the children, who really couldn't be expected to be clever enough, said they had seen it, and liked it.

Then Herbert got an idea. He wondered if Binkle would sell it to him. He thought he would love to have a picture with himself in, especially one that would tell him which of his visitors were clever and which were stupid. So he went up to

Heather Cottage and asked Binkle.

'I don't want to *sell* it,' said Binkle. 'I've got a lot of money just now. But I'll give it to you in exchange for six of your biggest cabbages, Herbert Hedgehog.'

Now, Herbert was very proud of his cabbages and he nearly said no. But then he thought of the extraordinary magic of Binkle's picture and he said yes.

'I'll bring the cabbages tonight,' he said, and ran off.

That evening he gave Binkle his six finest cabbages, and received in return Binkle's famous 'picture'. He carried it proudly off and hung it up in the dining room of his little yellow house.

Everybody was very envious. Whenever they went to call at Herbert's house, he let them have a look at it, and though nobody ever saw anything on the wall but an empty canvas, gradually getting dirty, none of them said anything but, 'Wonderful picture, Herbert! Wonderful! You're a lucky fellow to have it!'

Now, when Binkle and Flip had eaten all Herbert's

cabbages they went to call on him. He was sitting in his cottage, and Dilly, Mowdie Mole, Riggles Rat and Sammy Squirrel were at tea with him.

'Come on, come in,' called Herbert. 'Very pleased to see our famous artist!'

Binkle and Flip went in and sat down.

'There's your wonderful picture!' said Herbert, waving his pipe towards the wall.

Binkle looked – then he looked again – then he stared hard and rubbed his eyes.

'Herbert,' he said reproachfully, 'you've washed all my picture off the canvas! It's absolutely empty! Isn't it, Flip?'

'Quite,' said Flip. 'Oh, what a pity! Such a lovely picture too! Everybody said how blue the sky was! Oh, Herbert, how could you?'

Herbert looked as if he was going to have a fit. His little eyes grew red and his prickles stood up on end. He couldn't say a word, though he wanted to, terribly badly.

'I'm *surprised* at you, Herbert!' went on Binkle sadly. 'Why did you do it? Oh! I believe I know.

You wanted to make people say there was still a picture there, when there wasn't, so that you could laugh up your sleeve at them for pretending, in case anyone thought them stupid! Oh, Herbert, I didn't think it of you! My beautiful picture! All gone! All washed off! Not a trace left!'

Binkle took out his handkerchief, covered his eyes with it, pretended to sob, and walked out of the cottage, followed in a great hurry by Flip, who knew he would have to giggle very soon if he saw Herbert's astonished and indignant face much longer.

As soon as they had gone Herbert snatched down the picture, broke up the frame and put the whole thing in the fire. He saw through Binkle's trick very well indeed, but he knew that everyone would pretend he had washed off the picture, for no one would want to own up to how stupid they really *had been* in saying Binkle's empty canvas was a lovely picture.

'No one's ever to *mention* that picture again!' exploded Herbert Hedgehog, bristling with rage.

No one ever did – except Binkle and Flip, and

they *would* keep saying what a pity it was to have destroyed Binkle's lovely blue sky *and* Herbert Hedgehog's portrait.

'And who would have thought –' said Binkle to Flip that night – 'who *would* have thought that silly old pretend-picture could really show us how stupid everybody in Oak Tree Town was! All of them thought they were so clever, yet nobody was clever enough to see through my little trick! Dear, dear, Oak Tree Town isn't very good at telling the truth! But we *have* had some fun out of it!'

And they certainly had.

# Fairyland Folk

# THE ADVENTURES OF THE TOY SHIP

MARY and Timothy had a little ship. It had a fine blue sail, and its name, *Lucy Ann*, was painted on the side. The children often took it down to the stream to sail it, and it floated beautifully. It didn't turn over on its side as so many toy boats do – it sailed upright, just like a proper boat.

One day when Mary and Timothy were sailing the *Lucy Ann*, the string broke.

Oh dear! Down the stream it floated, faster and

faster, and the children ran after it. But the little boat kept to the middle of the stream and, no matter how they tried, the children could not reach it.

At last they could no longer run by the stream, for someone's big garden ran right down to the edge of the water, and a fence stood in their way. Very sad, the children watched as the *Lucy Ann* disappeared round a bend in the stream. They went back home, afraid that their ship would feel very lost without them.

So it did. The little ship tried its hardest to go back, but the stream took it along too fast. On and on it went until at last it came to rest beside a mossy bank. Its prow stuck into the soft earth and there it stayed. The little ship could move neither backwards nor forwards.

Night came, and the ship was astonished to see the moon in the sky, for before it had always spent the night in the toy cupboard. It did not know that there were such things as moon or stars. It stared up at the big silver moon and thought it was very beautiful.

Then suddenly, through the silence of the night, there came the sound of singing. On the opposite side of the stream, the little ship was surprised to see a great many twinkling lights, like tiny Japanese lanterns, shining in rainbow colours through the darkness.

It heard a lot of little voices, and saw a great number of fairy folk, all most excited. They were dressed in beautiful costumes – rose-petal waistcoats edged with diamond dewdrops, daffodil skirts and bluebell waistcoats.

Then, as the little boat watched in amazement, a ring of toadstools sprang up, and the pixies laid little white cloths on them for tables. They set out plates and glasses, and tiny knives and forks. Then they put out some tiny golden chairs for a group of pixies who carried musical instruments.

*These must be the fairy folk that Mary and Timothy sometimes talked about*, thought the ship to itself. Then it saw a small boat, smaller than itself, on the opposite side of the stream, and a pixie man got into it.

Quite nearby, on the top of its own mossy bank, the ship saw more fairy folk. They had with them all sorts of good things to eat! Honey cakes, flower biscuits, blue jellies with pink ice cream on the top, lemonade made of dew, special blancmanges in the shape of birds and animals, and many other good things.

They carried these goodies in woven baskets and on silver dishes. They were waiting for the other little boat to fetch them across the stream, so that they might lay out their food on the ring of toadstool tables.

'Hey! Little boat, come and fetch us!' they cried to the boat on the other side. The pixie man in it began to row across. But suddenly a great fish popped up its head and made such a large wave that the pixie boat was filled with water and sank!

Oh, what a noise there was! How all the little folk shouted and cried in fear, when they saw their boat sink, and the pixie man in the water!

'Oh, no! The boat's sunk! Oh, look at the

boatman, is he safe? Oh, what shall we do now! We haven't another boat and all our lovely food is on the other side of the stream!'

Listening in dismay, the *Lucy Ann* suddenly had a grand idea! It could take the pixies to the other side with all their baskets and dishes! So it spoke up in its funny, watery voice. How all the fairy folk jumped when they heard it! One little pixie was so surprised that she dropped the dish she was carrying, and spilt blue jelly all over the grass.

'I will take you across the stream, if you know how to sail me,' said the little ship. 'Don't be frightened. I am only a toy ship, I cannot hurt you. I will be only too glad to be of help.'

The pixies ran to the little ship and chattered at the tops of their silvery voices. Yes, it would do beautifully! What luck that it happened to be there! If it hadn't, the party would have been spoilt – and the king and queen themselves were coming!

Soon, the pixies had loaded all their food on board and settled down. One of them sat at the front and guided the ship out into the moonlit stream.

How proud the little toy ship was! Never before had it had anything but dolls aboard, and they couldn't do anything but sit still and stare at the sky. But these little fairy folk chattered and laughed. They ran here and there across its decks, they leant over the side and tried to dip their fingers in the water. It was great fun for the little ship!

Out it went over the stream, sailing most beautifully. The wind filled its sails and it floated like a swan, proud and handsome.

The fairies on the other side cried out in delight – they were so grateful that the *Lucy Ann* had saved their party. And would you believe it, at that very moment the king and queen of Fairyland arrived, riding in their golden carriage?

They watched the little boat too, and how pleased they were to see it come safely to the bank. All the fairies cheered, and the ship's blue sail trembled with joy.

The *Lucy Ann* stayed by the bank to watch the party. It smiled to see the little folk dancing to their pixie music. And then the king and queen asked the little ship if it would take them for a sail up the stream in the moonlight. What an honour!

'Oh, Your Majesties, I would love to,' said the ship. 'But the stream is so strong that I find it difficult to sail against it.'

'We will help you by a magic spell,' said the king. 'You shall take us far up the stream, to the place where the flowers grow, and when we are tired of sailing our butterfly carriage will bring us home. Ho there, pixies, bid our carriage follow us up the stream!'

The king and queen stepped into the boat and off it went, sailing easily against the current, for the king had used his magic to help the ship.

How enjoyable it was, sailing along in the moonlight! The little ship had never felt so happy or so proud – after all, it was carrying the king and queen of Fairyland.

It was a beautiful night. On either side, the banks were lined with trees that shone silver in the moonlight, and the little waves on the stream looked like silver too.

Bats fluttered silently overhead and the old owl hooted to them as he flew by. All around them the little ship fancied it could hear the sound of fairy voices singing a gentle lullaby. It was a most exciting journey.

After a lovely long sail the king spoke to the little ship once more.

'We will land now,' he said. 'Draw in to the bank, little ship. See where our butterfly carriage awaits us!'

The ship saw a beautiful carriage drawn by four yellow butterflies. It was waiting by a fence on the bank, overhung with beautiful roses.

The *Lucy Ann* sailed to the side and waited there while the king and queen got out. Then, as it looked about, the little ship gave a glad cry.

'Why! This is where Mary and Timothy played with me this morning!' it said. 'If only I could stay here, then they might find me in the morning!'

'Of course you shall stay here,' said the king. 'I will tie you to a stick.'

So he tied the little ship tightly to a twig in the

bank. The king then said goodbye and thanked the ship very much for all its help.

'I will turn your sail into a silver one, in reward for your kindness,' said the queen. In a trice the ship's blue sail became one of glittering silver thread. It was really splendid. Then the king and queen mounted their butterfly carriage and off they rode in the moonlight.

Soon it was dawn. The ship slept for a little while, and then woke up. It was proud of its glittering silver sail, and it longed for Mary and Timothy to come down to the stream to see it.

The children came running down before breakfast – and how they stared when they saw the little toy ship!

'Look at that beautiful ship!' cried Mary. 'Where did it come from? It's just like ours, only it has a silver sail!'

'I wonder who tied it to that stick,' said Timothy, puzzled. 'Nobody comes down here but us.'

'Ooh, look, Timothy – it *is* our ship! It's called *Lucy Ann*!' cried Mary in excitement. 'See, its name is on the side so it *must* be ours. But how did it get its beautiful sail, and who tied it up here for us to find?'

'The fairies must have had a hand in it,' said Timothy. 'And see, Mary – this proves it! Look at those two tiny cakes on the deck there! The fairies used our ship last night, and one of them dropped those cakes! Did you ever see such tiny things? Shall we eat them?'

'Yes – but let's save them till tonight, then maybe we'll see the fairies too!' cried Mary. They took their ship from the water and ran to tell Mummy all about it. She was so surprised to see its silver sail!

The ship was glad to be back in the toy cupboard. And how it enjoyed itself telling all the other toys of its adventures!

Mary and Timothy are going to eat those pixie cakes tonight. I do wonder what will happen, don't you?

# THE GOSSAMER ELF

EVERYBODY knew the Gossamer Elf. She was the cleverest dressmaker in the whole of Fairyland. You should have seen the dresses and cloaks she made!

'I think her autumn clothes are the best,' said Winks. 'She made me a lovely dress last October of a red creeper leaf. I went to lots of parties in it.'

'She made me a cloak out of a pair of beech leaves,' said Feefo. 'It was a golden cloak, the

prettiest I ever had.'

'Her stitches are the finest I ever saw,' said Tiptoe. 'Well, they're so fine I can't see them! Once I thought that the Gossamer Elf didn't sew our frocks at all, but just made them by magic. She doesn't though; I've seen her sewing away with a tiny, tiny needle.'

'Ah, but have you seen her thread?' said Winks. 'It's so fine and so strong that once she's put a stitch into a frock, it never comes undone.'

'What does she use for thread?' said Feefo. 'I'd like to get some. I'll go and ask her.'

So she went to call on the Gossamer Elf. But the elf was out. She had left her door open and Feefo went inside. On a shelf she saw reels upon reels – but they were all empty. Not one reel had any thread on it. How strange!

Soon the Gossamer Elf came in. Feefo ran to her. 'I've come to ask you something. Where do you get your fine thread? I can't see any on your reels.'

The Gossamer Elf smiled. 'No – my reels are all empty now,' she said. 'But soon they will be filled again with the finest, silkiest thread. I always get my thread at this time of year, you know.'

'Where from?' asked Feefo. 'Can I get some too? Do let me. Take me with you and I'll buy some.'

'I don't buy it,' said the elf. 'Yes, you can come with me if you like. I'm starting out tomorrow morning at dawn. You can carry some of my empty reels with you. That will be a help.'

So Feefo and the Gossamer Elf set out at dawn. They went to the fields. It was a lovely morning, and the sun shone softly from a blue sky.

'It's gossamer time now,' said the elf. 'Did you know that? Soon the air will be full of fine silken threads that will stretch across the fields everywhere. See – you can spy some already, gleaming in the sun.'

Feefo looked. Yes – she could see some fine, long threads stretching from the hedge above high up into the air. Soon there would be plenty of them.

'But what are those silky threads?' said Feefo in wonder. 'Where do they come from? Who makes them?'

'Climb up the hedge with me and I'll show you,'

said the elf. 'Some very small friends of mine make them. We'll watch them.'

They climbed up the hedge together, using the prickles on the wild rose stems as steps. They soon got high up in the hedge. Then Feefo saw around her many tiny spiders – young ones, not much more than babies.

Some stood on leaves, some clung to stems, and all of them were doing the same thing. They were sending out long silken threads from underneath their bodies.

'They have their silk spinnerets there,' said the elf. 'Big spiders have too. They take the thread from their spinnerets. Watch that tiny spider. See the long thread coming out, and waving in the air?'

'Oh, yes,' said Feefo in surprise. She saw dozens of tiny spiders all doing the same thing. 'But why are they all doing this, elf? It seems very queer to me. They are not spinning webs.'

'No, they are going out into the world to seek their fortunes,' said the elf. 'Each baby spider wants to leave the place where he was born. He wants to journey far away and find his own place to live. So he is sending out a long, long thread into the air – and then, when he has a long enough line, he will let the wind take him off into the air with his gossamer thread – and, like a tiny parachutist, he will soar over the world, and then drop gently to ground.'

'Goodness me!' said Feefo, astonished. 'Look, there goes one, elf! Away he goes on the wind.'

The tiny spider had let go his hold of the leaf, and now, swinging gently on the end of his gossamer thread he let himself be carried away on the breeze, exactly like a tiny parachutist. Feefo and the elf watched him soaring away, until he could no longer be seen.

'They're all doing it, all the baby spiders!' cried Feefo in delight. 'Oh, look at them swinging away on their threads. The wind blows the threads away and the spiders go with them!'

They watched the curious sight for a little while. Then Feefo turned to the elf. 'But, elf,' she said, 'surely you don't take their threads away from the tiny spiders? That would be a most unkind thing to do.'

'Of course I don't,' said the elf. 'How could you

207

think I'd do that? No – once the spiders have made their journey and landed safely somewhere, they don't want their threads any more. So I collect them on my reels, you see. I wind them up carefully, and soon have all my reels full for my year's work.'

'Well, what a good idea,' cried Feefo. 'Look – there comes a spider from far away; see him swinging down on the end of his line? Here he is, just beside us. Little spider, what an adventure you've had!'

'May I take your thread please, if you don't want it any more?' asked the Gossamer Elf politely. 'Oh, thank you. What a nice long one!'

She began to wind the gossamer round and round her reel. Soon the reel was full. The spider ran off to find himself a nice new home under a leaf. Maybe he would catch plenty of flies there, he thought. Soon he would spin a fine web, and wait for his dinner to come along and fly into it.

Another spider landed a little further down. Feefo ran to him. As soon as he had cast off his gossamer she began to wind it round and round the reel she carried. *What fun this is!* she thought. *Now I know*

*why the Gossamer Elf has her name. How clever she is to think of this idea!*

Day after day, early in the morning, Feefo and the Gossamer Elf came out together, and waited for the adventuring spiders to land near them on their gossamer lines. Soon they had dozens and dozens of reels full of the fine silken thread.

'There. We've got enough!' said the elf at last. 'Now I shall wait for the leaves to change colour and soon I shall be hard at work again making winter dresses and cloaks and sewing them with the gossamer thread given me by the tiny spiders. I shall be very busy indeed this winter!'

So she is. She is making coats of blackberry leaves, crimson, yellow and pink; frocks of golden hazel leaves, trimmed with berries and cloaks of brilliant cherry leaves. You should see them! But you can't see her stitches – they are made of the gossamer from the spiders.

Have you ever seen it? You really must. You can take some too, if you want, for the spiders won't need it again.

# FIREWORKS IN FAIRYLAND

ONCE upon a time there lived in Fairyland a number of little workmen, all dressed in bright green. They had very long legs and very sleepy eyes, and they sat in the grass all day to do their work.

They were the fairies' knife grinders, and whenever a fairy wanted her knife sharpened you could hear the *buzz-z-z* of the blunt knife held against the little grindstone that each workman had by him.

The fairies used to bring their knives each morning

early, and then, as they were being sharpened, they sat on toadstools and talked.

'The North Wind is in a terrible temper today,' said one. 'I met him just now.'

'Ah!' said one of the knife grinders. '*I* know why. It's because the late roses came out yesterday in the queen's garden, and she won't let the North Wind blow till they're over!'

'And he says he *must* blow, else he'll burst himself with keeping all his breath in,' went on another workman, stopping his grinding because he was so interested.

'Yesterday I saw Hoo, the white owl, and he told me a lovely story about those three naughty little gnomes, Ding, Dong and Dell,' began another fairy.

'Oh, do tell us!' begged all the workmen, stopping work at once to listen.

The fairy told them the story, and the workmen forgot all about their knives. When the story came to an end the sun was high in the sky, and it was nearly twelve o'clock.

'Oh, I'm so sleepy!' yawned a knife grinder, lying down on his back.

'I *can't* finish these knives!' said another, and fell asleep beside his grindstone.

There those lazy little workmen slept soundly until four o'clock, when the fairy queen happened to come along, bringing a crowd of elves with her.

'Oh, Your Majesty, look here!' cried one, pointing to a sleeping workman. 'He's fast asleep, and it's only four o'clock!'

'How disgraceful!' exclaimed the queen. 'And look at all those blunt knives! They ought to have been sharpened long ago! Does this often happen?'

'We don't know,' answered the elves, 'but Hoo, the white owl, lives near here, and could tell you.'

So Hoo was called and flew silently down to the queen.

'Yes, Your Majesty,' he said in answer to her question, 'they are good little workmen, but terribly lazy. They are forever talking with the fairies, and going to sleep any hour of the day.'

'Wake them up,' commanded the queen to her

213

elves. 'I can't stop to scold them, but you may stay behind and do it for me.'

The queen flew on and left some of her elves behind.

'We'll give them a fright,' whispered the elves. Then each elf flew down beside a workman and shouted a most tremendous shout in his ear. Then, quick as lightning, they hid themselves behind toadstools.

You should have seen those workmen jump! They all woke up at once, nearly jumped out of their skins and looked all around in great terror.

'What was it?' they all cried.

Out came the elves from behind the toadstools, looking very stern.

'The queen has just passed,' they said, 'and found you all asleep with your work not done. She is very cross indeed!'

But the workmen hardly listened. 'Was it *you* who woke us up like that?' they asked, looking very fierce.

'Yes, it was, and it serves you right!' answered the elves.

'Then you are very unkind, and we'll pull your ears!' shouted the workmen, rushing at the elves. But, quick as thought, they spread their wings and flew away, laughing at the angry little knife grinders.

'It's a *shame*!' stormed one. 'Those horrid little elves are *always* playing tricks on us and making us jump!'

'Can't we pay them back somehow and give *them* a fright?' asked another.

'Yes, let's! How could we make them jump just like they made us?'

'I've got a glorious idea!' said another. 'Let's go to the world of boys and girls and get some fireworks. It's November the fifth tomorrow and there will be plenty about.'

'Yes, and go to the palace and play tricks on those elves with them!' cried all the other workmen, looking really excited.

So it was all arranged. Two workmen were sent off to get rockets, Catherine wheels, Golden Rain, and Jumping Squibs from our world. They soon came back with a big sack full of them, and the

knife grinders made all their plans.

Next morning a message came to them from the queen, saying they must all go to the palace that day, as she was holding a great party and dance for her elves, and wanted all the knives sharpened.

'That's better still!' cried the workmen, and hurried off at once.

They sharpened all the knives very quickly and then asked if they could help lay the table for the feast, and polish the floor for the dancing.

'Certainly!' answered the head steward. 'You are very good to help us.'

So those knife grinders slipped into the banqueting hall, and began preparing their tricks. They put some crackers in the dishes of sweets and chocolates and some in the middle of a big ice-cream pudding.

'I'm going to put Golden Rain fireworks among all these flowers round the hall!' called a busy workman. 'The elves always smell the flowers!'

'And I'm pinning Catherine wheels on to the wall!' chuckled another. 'The elves won't know what they are, and they'll be sure to poke about and see!'

'Look, do look! I've had a glorious idea! I've tied rockets to the front legs of every chair! Won't those elves jump?' called another knife grinder, looking most delighted.

'Isn't it *lovely*? Won't they be cross? They *will* be sorry they made us jump!' called all the workmen.

'Now we'd better hide somewhere and watch. We'll go behind those big curtains. Have you all got squibs in your pockets?' asked the biggest workman.

'Yes,' answered the rest.

'Now, all be quiet while I say some magic. We shall have to use some to make the fireworks go off directly anyone touches them.'

Everyone was quiet, and the leader sang some queer words.

'There!' he said. 'Now, directly anyone *touches* those hidden fireworks, they'll all go off – bang! Let's go and hide.'

The knife grinders ran behind the long curtains, and there they waited till the guests came in to the party.

Soon the elves arrived, all in beautiful dresses and

217

shiny wings. Then came the queen, and gave the signal for the feast to begin.

Everything went well until an elf asked for some ice-cream pudding. For directly the head steward began to put a spoon into it, there came a most tremendous noise!

CRACK! SPLUTTER-CRACK! BANG!

It was the cracker inside the pudding, gone off as soon as it was touched!

'Oh, oh! What is it?' gasped the head steward, looking very astonished.

Then suddenly—

CRACK! BANG! CRACK!

The elves were helping themselves to chocolates and sweets, and the crackers in the dishes were exploding!

How those elves jumped! And how the naughty little workmen laughed behind the curtain.

'Someone has been playing tricks,' said the queen, looking rather stern. 'If you have all finished, get down, and we will start dancing.'

The elves got down, and went into the dancing

hall. The workmen followed, making sure no one saw them, and hid behind the curtains there.

'What glorious flowers!' cried the elves, and bent to smell the wonderful roses round the walls.

*Fizzle-fizzle-fizz! Whizz-z-z!*

Out shot Golden Rain, directly the fairies smelt the roses!

'Oh, what is it?' they cried, falling over one another in their haste to get away. 'It must be some new sort of caterpillar! Ugh, how horrid!'

'Yes, and what are those funny curly things on the walls?' asked the queen.

An elf went up to a Catherine wheel and poked it with his finger.

*Whirr-r-r-r! Whirr-r-r-r!*

The wheel spun round and round and shot off sparks!

'Oh, it's alive! It's alive! What is it, what is it?' shouted the elves, crowding together in frightened astonishment.

'Never mind,' said the queen, looking sterner than ever. 'Begin your dancing.'

The elves began dancing round the room.

'Throw your Jumping Squibs on the floor!' whispered the biggest workman. 'That will make the elves jump!'

Quickly the squibs were thrown on the floor of the hall.

CRACK! SPLUTTER-JUMP! CRACK! JUMP!

Those squibs were jumping all over the place!

'Oh! Get off my toe, you horrid thing!'

'Goodness me! Go away, go away!'

'Oh, oh, what are they? They jump at us and won't let us dance!'

The elves were really frightened.

'Go and sit down,' commanded the queen, 'and I will find out who has done these naughty things.'

The elves went to the chairs round the hall and sat down.

*Whizz-z-z! Whoosh-sh-sh!* BANG!

All the rockets tied to the chairs shot up in the air directly they were touched by the elves!

'Oh, oh!' cried the elves, nearly jumping out of their skins with fright.

221

'Keep where you are,' called the queen, 'and see what else happens.'

Nothing happened, and the elves began to feel more comfortable.

'Lord High Chamberlain,' commanded the queen in a dreadfully stern voice, 'go and look behind those curtains over there.'

The Lord High Chamberlain stepped across and pulled the curtains aside.

And there were all the naughty little green workmen, looking very frightened indeed!

'Come here,' said the queen.

They all came and stood in front of her throne.

'What do you mean by playing such naughty tricks on my elves?' she demanded.

'Please, Your Majesty, they made *us* jump the other day, so we thought we'd make *them* jump,' answered the biggest workman.

'You know quite well that that's not the right thing to do at all,' said the queen. 'I am quite ashamed of you. You are not fit to be in Fairyland. You have spoilt our party and frightened all my elves.'

'Oh, please, we *are* sorry now,' sobbed the workmen, feeling very miserable.

'You don't do your work well and you are lazy,' said the queen. 'I think it would do *you* good to do some jumping and stretch those long legs of yours a bit. I am going to punish you, and perhaps you will remember another time that I will have no one in my kingdom who does not do his work well and beautifully.'

'*Please* let us sharpen the fairies' knives for them,' begged the knife grinders. 'We really *will* do it beautifully now.'

'Very well, you may still do that,' said the queen, 'and as you are so fond of making people jump, you had better jump a lot too.'

She waved her wand.

And every little workman there turned into a green grasshopper!

'Go into the fields,' said the queen, 'and do your work properly.'

All the green grasshoppers turned to go, stretched their long legs and *jumped* out of the hall! Hop

223

and a jump, and a jump, and out they went into the fields.

They still sharpen the fairies' knives for them, and you can hear their grindstones buzzing in the summer somewhere down in the grass. And when you see them hopping you will know why it is they jump instead of run!

Fireworks are forbidden in Fairyland now, and I really don't wonder at it, do you?

# The Rose that Didn't Grow

ONCE upon a time the king of Fairyland had a wonderful rose garden.

As he walked through it one day, examining all the buds and smelling all the full-blown roses, he sighed.

'We have plenty of red roses and plenty of pink and white,' he said to the head gardener, 'and I know them all, every one. Don't you think it's about time we had some new kinds?'

'Your Majesty,' answered the head gardener, 'you already have all the kinds there are. There are no new roses to be had in all Fairyland.'

'Well, that's ridiculous,' said the king. 'Why, in the world of boys and girls people are *always* inventing new roses. Why can't *we* invent some new sorts? I'd like a yellow rose. We've red and white, pink and cream, but not a single yellow one!'

'Well, Your Majesty,' suggested the gardener, 'why don't you send out a royal proclamation, asking everyone to set their wits to work and grow some new kinds of roses? It's just the sort of thing the elves and fairies love to do!'

'Good! Splendid idea!' cried the king. 'I'll go and do it at once!' and away he hurried into the palace, and called for pen and ink and paper.

Then, because he was an excellent writer, the king wrote out the proclamation himself. When it was finished he blotted it carefully and gave it to the Lord High Chamberlain.

'Make this proclamation known through the kingdom,' he ordered.

'Yes, Your Majesty,' answered the chamberlain, and hurried off.

In a little while all the heralds of Fairyland were blowing their trumpets, and calling out the king's proclamation to crowds of excited fairies.

'Oyez, oyez, oyez!' they called in their clear, silvery voices. 'The king of Fairyland offers a reward to whomsoever will bring him the most beautiful new yellow rose. The winner will be made Grand Keeper of all the Flowers. Oyez, oyez, oyez!'

Then began such an excitement in Fairyland! Pixies and elves, gnomes and fairies hurried to their gardens to see if they could, by help of what magic they knew, change the roses growing there into beautiful yellow ones.

'I'm going to look up spells in an old book of magic I've got!' said one, turning out a cupboard to find it. She turned over page after page of the book until she came to the word 'yellow'.

'To make anything change its colour to yellow, dance lightly on one foot four times round the object, morning and evening, chanting the magic word:

227

Fala-gari-oona-ree!' cried the fairy, reading from the book.

So morning and evening the fairy could be seen lightly dancing on one foot and singing to the big red rose tree in her garden. Day by day it changed its colour little by little, and the fairy was most excited.

A little elf had a great idea. *If I water my rose tree with something yellow, that will turn the flowers yellow!* he thought, and he hunted about for something golden.

At last he made a mixture of early-morning sunshine and amber-yellow dewdrops, and every day he watered his rose tree with them, until the rosebuds began to look as yellow as the sunbeams.

The pixies, who had a splendid rose garden of their own, met together to consult as to what plan *they* follow.

'I know,' cried one. 'Let's mix a strong and powerful yellow paint, and get Artis, who paints exquisitely, to colour all our white roses yellow for us! If the king says a magic spell over them, the colour will stay on always, and next year's flowers will be yellow too!'

'Splendid!' cried the rest. 'Now, let's all go and find something to make the paint.' Off they went, into all the corners of Fairyland.

One scooped the yellow sunshine from the tops of pools at sunrise. Another begged the brimstone butterfly for some of the yellow dust on his wings. And a third had a splendid idea. He went about with a long silver spoon, and took the gold that lies in the heart of daffodils.

Many other pixies brought yellow powders and yellow dust for the paint, and when they were all ready, they were shaken into a glass jar, and stirred up with frosted cobwebs to make them sticky. The yellow fairy paint gleamed through the glass, a glorious colour that glistened and shone curiously.

'Artis! Artis!' called the excited pixies. 'Come here quickly, and look!'

Artis came forward slowly. He was a queer little dreamy fairy, with big ears and deep brown eyes that saw many things no other fairy could see.

He carried a big palette and many brushes.

'What a beautiful colour!' he cried in astonishment as he saw the glass jar. 'Oh, give me some to use for my painting!'

'Yes, we will, if you'll do something for us!' said the pixies. 'See, we want you to paint our white roses yellow for us. Will you?'

'Of course I will,' promised Artis, picking up the jar. 'I'll begin at once. I'd *love* to do that!' and off he hurried into the pixie rose garden. He settled himself down by the wall, in the shade, and carefully began to paint a large rosebud.

Now over the wall, in a little higgledy-piggledy house, lived a tiny gnome. His name was Acaulis, and he was very excited when he heard that the king wanted a yellow rose.

'I'll look at the rose tree in my garden,' he said to himself, and hurried home to see.

But alas! His rose tree was dead!

'Oh dear! Oh dear!' sighed Acaulis. '*Now* what shall I do? I *must* take a yellow rose to the king somehow or other!'

He sat and thought for a long time – and then, he remembered he had many a time done a good turn to the Simple Witch, who lived away in the hills, so he decided to go and ask her help.

When he arrived at her cottage she was busy undoing a purple packet.

'Good morning,' she said. 'I know what you want, so don't bother to tell me. I'll help you if I can.'

'Good morning, and thank you,' answered Acaulis politely, quite used to the queer ways of the witch.

'Now, look,' said the Simple Witch suddenly. 'Here are some yellow seeds from the Land of Makebelieve. I am going to give you one, Acaulis, for you have often been kind to me. If you follow all my directions carefully, you will have a beautiful yellow rose, far more beautiful in colour, shape and smell than any other.'

'You are very kind indeed,' said Acaulis gratefully. 'Tell me what I must do.'

The Simple Witch threw one of the yellow seeds into a pot over the fire, and stirred it about, while she chanted a magic song.

231

'*Sweet and mellow,*
*Rich and yellow;*
*Even so*
*May you grow,*'

sang the witch. Then she picked out the seed again and gave it to Acaulis.

'Plant it,' she said. 'Water it with honey and dew on each Friday evening just before sunset. If you miss watering it, it will not grow properly. Goodbye.'

'Goodbye,' said Acaulis gratefully, and ran off as fast as he could to plant the magic seed.

He planted it, and then went to buy a pot of honey from the Bee-Woman, so that when Friday came he could water it with dew and honey.

One day he heard Artis singing, and he popped his head over the wall of the pixie rose garden.

'Hallo, Artis!' he called. 'What are you doing?'

'Painting white roses yellow!' answered Artis. 'See what a lot I've done!'

'How beautiful they are!' marvelled Acaulis. 'You do paint splendidly, Artis!'

After that the little gnome sat on the wall every day and talked to Artis. The two soon became very fond of one another, for both were merry, sunny little creatures.

On the first Friday evening Acaulis mixed dew and honey together and carefully watered the tiny little plant growing from his seed. 'I *do* hope it will be beautiful,' said Acaulis to himself, 'for I would so love to be Grand Keeper of all the Flowers!'

On the second Friday evening, just as Acaulis was preparing the dew and honey, there came a knock at his door.

'Acaulis, Acaulis! Come quickly! Misty-May has caught her wing in a bramble, and she wants you to get it free for her!' cried a voice.

'Oh, I *can't* come!' answered Acaulis. 'I *must* water my rose plant!'

'*Do* come! *Do* come!' begged the voice.

Kind-hearted Acaulis put down the honeypot and ran out to the woods to help Misty-May.

But alas! When he returned the sun had set, and it was too late to water his plant!

'Oh, now it won't grow, it won't grow!' wept Acaulis. Then he dried his eyes. 'Never mind. Perhaps if I give it *two* lots of honey and dew next Friday it won't matter,' he decided.

All that week the plant did not grow a single inch, and Acaulis was very upset. On the next Friday, as he was hurrying home to water his plant, he met his friend Grey-Ears, the rabbit, carrying a load of green moon-beads to the queen's dressmaker.

'We're going the same way, Grey-Ears,' said Acaulis. 'Let me carry your load for you for a little while.'

'Thank you very much,' said Grey-Ears, and gave the moon-beads to Acaulis.

They hurried along till suddenly Acaulis tripped over a tree stump and – clitter-clatter, clitter-clatter! All the green moon-beads rolled here, there and everywhere.

'Oh, they'll be lost! Whatever shall I do?' cried Grey-Ears in despair.

'I'm *dreadfully* sorry!' said poor little Acaulis. 'I'll pick them all up for you, really I will.'

And he did. But by the time he had hunted under all the leaves and in all the moss the sun had set, and another Friday evening had gone by without his precious plant being watered. Acaulis was dreadfully upset.

'I'll stay home next Friday and make sure it is watered,' he said to himself.

So the next Friday he stayed at home. Just as he was getting down the little honeypot a pixie rushed in.

'Artis is ill! He has a terrible sore throat and he's got to eat pots and pots of honey to make him better. Have you got any to spare?'

'Oh dear! I *did* so want it; but never mind, take my honey for Artis,' said Acaulis with tears in his eyes, giving the precious pot of honey to the pixie. The pixie ran off, and Acaulis went out and watered his tiny plant with dew alone, though he knew that wouldn't do any good at all. But there wasn't enough time before sunset to get any more honey from the Bee-Woman.

The plant didn't grow at all. It had a funny little

collection of leaves growing all together and a few yellowish buds. Acaulis thought it was rather pretty, but a very poor specimen for a rose.

'Anyway, I'll take it to the king,' he decided. 'He might happen to like it.'

On the evening before the rose show a great rainstorm came. Acaulis peeped over the wall, and saw, to his dismay, that the drenching rain was

washing all the colour off the roses that Artis had painted so carefully. He hurriedly climbed over the wall, took off his cap and held it over one really beautiful yellow rose that the rain had hardly spoilt.

'This will save *one* of Artis's roses, anyhow,' said Acaulis, and stayed there till the rain had stopped, and the pixies came running out.

'Oh you *are* a good friend!' they cried to Acaulis. 'Artis will be so pleased to have one left. He was afraid they would all be spoilt for tomorrow. He couldn't come out because his throat isn't better; but he's going to the rose show tomorrow!'

Acaulis ran back to his cottage and dried himself. He felt quite sure Artis's rose would win the prize, and though he would have liked to be the Grand Keeper of all the Flowers himself, he felt there was no hope now, for his plant was so small and queer.

Next day, pixies, elves, gnomes and fairies crowded to the palace, bringing their pots and bowls of roses, each hoping to win the prize. They arranged them all in a row, and stood by them, waiting for the king.

'Oh, oh! Just look at Acaulis's plant!' laughed the fairies, pointing to it.

'Poor little plant!' said Acaulis. 'You might have grown beautifully if only I'd been able to water you. Never mind, I'll make you look ever so sweet and tidy, and perhaps the king will smile at you!'

So Acaulis arranged the leaves in a rosette round the buds, and bunched the buds together in the middle. One or two were out, and were a beautiful pale yellow, but very small and with only five petals.

Soon the king came along. He looked at the rose of the fairy who had danced round her bush morning and night.

'It is beautiful,' he said; 'but you have danced too much, and the rose is orange, not yellow.'

Then he looked at the rose of the elf who had watered his with sunshine and amber dewdrops.

'You have a beautiful rose,' he said, 'but see, your watering has turned the leaves and the stem yellow too, and that is ugly.'

He looked at many others, but not one did he

find that was perfect, until he came to the one that Artis had painted.

'Oh, how glorious!' he said. 'This is the one I shall choose.'

'Please, Your Majesty, it is painted,' said Artis. 'Will you say a magic spell over it, to make the paint stay always? And look, you haven't seen my friend's rose yet,' and he pointed to where Acaulis stood.

'What a queer, prim little rose!' said the king, looking at the tidy little plant. 'It isn't a *bit* like a rose, Acaulis, but it's a lovely yellow. Does it smell?'

'Yes, Your Majesty,' said Acaulis.

The king smelt it.

'Oh, Acaulis, it smells of the springtime,' cried the king excitedly. 'No flower has ever had such an exquisite, faint spring smell before! How *did* you grow such a flower?'

'Let *me* tell you, Your Majesty,' said Artis. And he not only told the king about the flower, but about all the kind deeds Acaulis had done instead of tending his plant as he wanted to.

'You are a good little gnome, Acaulis,' said the

king gently. 'I cannot give you the prize, because that must go to Artis; but because your flower is so dainty and smells of springtime, it shall be planted all over the country, to come out in the very early spring, and everyone will love it.'

Acaulis was tremendously pleased.

'What shall we call my flower?' he asked.

The king laughed. 'It's such a funny little prim and proper flower!' he said. 'Let's call it a primrose, shall we?'

And we still call the little yellow flower of the springtime the primrose, and if you are very sharp one day, you *might* see Acaulis arranging the leaves in a rosette, and enjoying the smell of springtime in the pale yellow blossoms of his precious flowers.

# MUDDY-ONE AND PRANKY

'THERE goes old Muddy-One!' said the big water snail. 'Look out, you young frogs.'

The little frogs swam up to the top of the pond at once. They were all afraid of Muddy-One. He was a large, ugly grub who lurked in the mud, and was always hungry.

Curly-Shell, the snail, wasn't at all afraid of Muddy-One. He had only to curl himself up in his hard shell whenever he spied the big grub, and

nobody could harm him then. But most of the other creatures in the pond were afraid of the ugly old grub.

Pranky, the water pixie, teased him dreadfully. He was a naughty little mischief, very quick and cheeky, and the names he called Muddy-One made all the snails and fishes laugh.

Muddy-One had been in the pond for a very long time. He had been small at first, but now he was big. He crawled about in the mud, and across his face he put a curious claw, which could shoot out and catch any little water creature in its pincers.

He didn't like being teased by Pranky. 'I can't help being ugly,' he would say. 'I didn't make myself. If I could have made myself, I would have given myself beautiful wings, and a gleaming body, and I wouldn't live down here in the slimy mud, but up in the sunshine. Sometimes I crawl up a water plant and look out of the water. Up there is a lovely world of light and warmth. I wish I belonged to it.'

'Well, you don't! An ugly creature like you wouldn't be allowed to live up in the bright sunshine,' said Pranky, and he poked the grub with a bit of stick. 'How lazy you are! Stir yourself! Gallop round the pond a bit.'

But Muddy-One wasn't very gallopy. He didn't like being poked with a stick, and he was angry with the unkind little pixie. But that only made Pranky call him ruder names than ever; so in the end Muddy-One buried himself deep down in the slime and tried to hide.

'He's ashamed of himself, and I don't wonder,' cried Pranky, poking his stick into the mud. 'What a pity somebody doesn't eat him. I'll find a big fish one day, Muddy-One, and send him along to eat you.'

'You shouldn't tease Muddy-One so,' said the big water snail. 'He doesn't do you any harm. You're unkind.'

Then Pranky swam to the snail and tried to pull him out of his shell. But he couldn't. So he wrote a rude sentence on the snail's shell and left him. He put 'I am a poor old slowcoach' all over the snail's shell, and the snail couldn't think why

everyone who met him laughed.

Pranky was just as much at home in the air as in the water. He was a lucky fellow, for he could run and swim. He was a fine-looking pixie too, and he knew it. He often used a shining dewdrop as a mirror, and looked at himself proudly in it.

One day the Princess Melisande thought she would give a party. Now, she lived high up on a hill above the clouds, so it was plain that every guest would have to fly there.

'I shall get my peacock butterfly to take me,' said Jinky the fairy.

'I'm going on Zoom the bumblebee,' said Tippy the goblin.

'I've got my lovely tiger moth,' said Twink the elf.

'What are *you* going on, Pranky?' asked Jinky.

'I shall ask the bluebottle to fly to Princess Melisande's with me,' said Pranky. 'He's such a lovely colour.'

But he couldn't ride the bluebottle because somebody saw it crawling with dirty feet over a baby's milk bottle, and the baby's mother killed it.

'He's a dirty, horrid bluebottle fly,' said the mother. 'He'll make the baby ill.'

So there was no bluebottle for the pixie to ride on. He *was* upset. 'Can I ride on Zoom with you?' he asked Tippy.

'No. He says you once sewed up the end of a foxglove flower when he had crawled inside, and he couldn't get out,' said Tippy. 'He doesn't like you.'

'Well, can I come on your butterfly?' Pranky asked Jinky.

'No, you can't. He isn't strong enough to carry two of us,' said Jinky. 'Why don't you get a dragonfly? He'd be very strong indeed, and very beautiful too. He would fly so fast that you'd be at the princess's in no time!'

'Oooh, yes! I'd love a dragonfly,' said Pranky, thinking how very grand he would feel riding such a lovely creature. 'But I haven't seen any yet. Where can I get one?'

'You'd better go and ask old Mother Wimple,' said Jinky. 'She knows all the insects well. She's

245

always mending their wings for them when they get torn. She could get you a dragonfly, I expect. But be polite to her, Pranky, because she's got a hot temper.'

Pranky flew off. He soon came to where Mother Wimple lived. She had a tiny house by the pond, and she was sitting outside it, busily patching the torn wing of a butterfly.

'Mother Wimple, I'm going to Princess Melisande's party,' said Pranky, sitting down beside her. 'And her palace is so high above the clouds that I've got to get some insect to take me. I want a dragonfly. Could you get me one, please?'

'You're very polite all of a sudden,' said old Mother Wimple, who had not heard very good tales of Pranky. 'You're one of those people who have very good manners when they want something, and can be very rude when they don't, aren't you?'

'Oh, *no*!' said Pranky, going rather red. 'No, I'm very well-behaved, Mother Wimple. Please do tell me if you can get me a dragonfly.'

'When is the party?' asked Mother Wimple.

'Tomorrow afternoon,' said Pranky.

'Come back an hour before you have to set off for the party, and I'll have here the finest dragonfly you ever saw,' said Mother Wimple.

Pranky flew off in the greatest delight. He was back in good time the next day, but he couldn't see any dragonfly.

'Be patient,' said Mother Wimple. 'You'll see him soon. Ah, here he comes.'

She pointed to a water plant whose stem came right up out of the pond. Up it was crawling the ugly old grub, Muddy-One. Pranky stared at him and then he stared at Mother Wimple.

'Why, that's no dragonfly – that's only ugly old Muddy-One!' he said.

'Oh, you know him, do you?' said Mother Wimple. 'Well now, you watch and see what is going to happen to him. You'll see something marvellous.'

Pranky watched. Muddy-One crawled right out of the water, and clung to the stem of the water plant, enjoying the hot sunshine.

Then, to the pixie's enormous surprise, the ugly old grub split his skin right down his back!

'Goodness gracious, look at that!' said Pranky. 'He's split himself. Has he eaten too much? I always told him he'd burst if he was so greedy.'

'Be quiet,' said Mother Wimple. 'Now look – he's split even further.'

Pranky watched in surprise. He saw that the ugly old grub was trying to creep out of his own skin. How extraordinary!

But what a different creature came out of the old skin! He had a long slender body that gleamed blue-green. He had crumpled wings. He had enormous eyes that shone in the sun, and six weak legs that clung to the water plant for safety.

'Why, Muddy-One's got wings,' cried Pranky. 'Look – he's spreading them out in the sun to dry them. They are long and lovely, and look at his beautiful blue-green body and eyes. Oh, Mother Wimple, he's not an ugly water grub any longer; he's a most *beautiful* dragonfly. It's magic, it's magic! Oh, how clever of you to make a dragonfly come out of Muddy's old skin.'

'I didn't,' said Mother Wimple. 'All dragonflies

live down in the mud as grubs for a long time. But when the right time comes, they creep up into the sunshine, take off their old skin and dart up into the air – gay, beautiful dragonflies!'

'Oh, I shall love to ride him,' cried Pranky.

Mother Wimple called to the dragonfly as he sat sunning his wings.

'Swift-One! Come here and take this pixie to Princess Melisande's.'

The dragonfly flew over to Mother Wimple and soared round her head, gleaming in the sun.

Pranky stood up in delight.

'Let me ride you, let me ride you!' he cried.

Swift-One the dragonfly flew just out of reach. 'What! Let you, a rude and ill-mannered pixie, ride me, the swiftest dragonfly in the world? Certainly not! I haven't forgotten how you teased me and the names you called me, you horrid little pixie!'

'That's not the way to talk, Swift-One,' said Mother Wimple sternly. 'I have promised Pranky that he shall ride you. Come down, so that he may get on your back.'

Swift-One darted down, and Pranky leapt on to his back. The dragonfly soared high in the air at such a pace that Pranky's breath was almost taken away. But then Swift-One began to play tricks.

He stopped suddenly in mid-air, and Pranky almost shot over his head. He flew upside down, and Pranky nearly fell off. He darted down to the surface of the pond and made the pixie get his feet wet. He teased Pranky just as much as Pranky had once teased him down in the pond.

Then he turned over and over and over in the air, and at last, the pixie, too giddy to hold on any longer, fell off and flew down to the ground, landing beside Mother Wimple with a bump.

He began to cry when he saw the dragonfly darting away at top speed.

Mother Wimple laughed. 'It serves you right,' she said. 'I thought he would play a few tricks on you, if he had the chance. Cry, Pranky, cry! Perhaps you will learn now not to make fun of ugly, slow creatures. You never know when they are going to change into beautiful, swift-flying things that will tip you off their backs.'

'I c-c-c-can't go to the party now,' wept Pranky. 'Tippy's gone by on his butterfly, and Jinky's gone on Zoom the bumblebee, but I've got no one to take *me*!'

He went home, very sorry for himself. And all that August and September he had to keep a sharp lookout for Swift-One, because the dragonfly flew down to nip the bad little pixie whenever he saw him.

Have you seen Swift-One, the dragonfly? Look out for him. He's beautiful.

# PINKITY AND OLD MOTHER RIBBONY ROSE

ONCE upon a time there lived an old witch called Mother Ribbony Rose. She kept a shop just on the borders of Fairyland, and because she sold such lovely things, the fairies allowed her to live there in peace.

She was very, very old, and very, very clever, but she wasn't very good. She was never kind to her neighbour, the Bee-Woman, and never helped the Balloon-Man, who lived across the road, and who was often very poor indeed when no one came to buy his pretty balloons.

But her shop was simply lovely. She sold ribbons, but they weren't just ordinary ribbons. There were blue ribbons, made of the mist that hangs over faraway hills, and sea-green ribbons embroidered with the diamond sparkles that glitter on sunny water. There were big broad ribbons of shiny silk, and tiny delicate ribbons of frosted spider's thread, and wonderful ribbons that tied their own bows.

The fairies and elves loved Mother Ribbony Rose's shop, and often used to come and buy there whenever a fairy dance was going to be held and they wanted pretty things to wear.

One day Mother Ribbony Rose was very busy indeed.

'Good morning, Fairy Jasmin,' she said, as a tall fairy, dressed in yellow, came into her shop. 'What can I get you today?'

'Good morning, Mother Ribbony Rose,' answered Jasmin politely. She didn't like the old witch a bit,

but that didn't make any difference; she was always polite to her. 'I would like to see the newest yellow ribbon you have, please, to match the dress I've got on today.'

Mother Ribbony Rose pulled out a drawer full of yellow ribbons. Daffodil-yellows, orange-yellows, primrose-yellows, and all shining like gold.

'Here's a beauty!' said she, taking up a broad ribbon. 'Would you like that?'

'No, thank you,' answered Jasmin. 'I want something narrower.'

The witch pulled out another drawer and scattered the ribbons on the counter.

'Ah, here's one I like ever so!' exclaimed Jasmin, lifting up a long thin piece of yellow ribbon, just the colour of her dress. 'How much is it?'

'Two pieces of gold,' answered Mother Ribbony Rose.

'Oh dear, you're terribly expensive,' sighed Jasmin as she paid the money and took the ribbon.

Mother Ribbony Rose looked at all the dozens of ribbons scattered over the counter.

'Pinkity, Pinkity, Pinkity,' she called in a sharp voice.

Out of the back of the shop came a tiny gnome. 'Roll up all these ribbons quickly, before anyone else comes in,' ordered Mother Ribbony Rose, going into the garden.

Pinkity began rolling them up one by one. He did it beautifully, and so quickly that it was a marvel to watch him.

When all the ribbons were done, he went to the window and looked out. He saw fairies, gnomes and pixies playing in the fields and meadows.

'Oh dear, dear, dear!' suddenly said Pinkity in a woebegone voice. 'How I would love to go and play with the fairies. I'm so *tired* of rolling up ribbons.' A large tear rolled down his cheek, and dropped with a splash on the floor.

'What's the matter, Pinkity?' suddenly asked a little voice.

Pinkity jumped and looked round. He saw a tiny fairy who had come into the shop and was waiting to be served.

'I'm so tired of doing nothing but roll up ribbons all day,' explained Pinkity.

'Well, why don't you do something else?' asked the fairy.

'That's the worst of it. I've never done anything else all my life but roll up ribbons in Mother Ribbony's shop, and I *can't* do anything else. I can't paint, I can't dance, and I can't sing! All the other fairies would laugh at me if I went to play with them, for I wouldn't even know *how* to play!' sobbed Pinkity.

'Oh, yes, you would! Come and try,' said the little fairy, feeling very sorry for the lonely little gnome.

'Come and try! Come and try *what*?' suddenly said Mother Ribbony's voice, as she came in at the door.

'I was just asking Pinkity if he would come and play with us,' answered the little fairy, feeling rather afraid of the witch's cross looks.

Mother Ribbony Rose snorted.

'Pinkity belongs to *me*,' she said, 'and he's much too busy in the shop, rolling up my beautiful ribbons all day, to have time to go and play with *you*. Besides, no one is allowed in Fairyland unless they can do some sort of work, and Pinkity can do nothing but roll up ribbons! I'm the only person who would keep him for that, for no one in Fairyland keeps a ribbon shop.' And the old witch pulled one of Pinkity's big ears.

'I should run away,' whispered the little fairy to Pinkity when her back was turned.

'I wish I could! But I've nowhere to run to!' whispered back Pinkity in despair.

At that moment there came the sound of carriage wheels down the cobbled street, and old Mother Ribbony Rose poked her head out to see who it was.

'Mercy on us! It's the Lord High Chancellor of Fairyland, and he's coming here! Make haste, Pinkity, and get a chair for him!' cried the old witch in a great flurry.

Sure enough it was.

The chancellor strode into the shop, very tall and handsome, and sat down in the chair.

'Good morning,' he said. 'The king and queen

are holding a dance tonight, and they are going to make the wood gay with ribbons and hang fairy lamps on them. The queen has asked me to come and choose the ribbons for her. Will you show me some, please?'

'Certainly, certainly, Your Highness!' answered Mother Ribbony Rose, pulling out drawer after drawer of lovely ribbons. Pinkity sighed as he watched her unroll ribbon after ribbon, and show it to the chancellor.

*Oh dear! I'm sure it will take me hours and hours to roll up all that ribbon!* he thought to himself sadly.

'This is wonderful ribbon!' said the chancellor admiringly. 'I'll have fifty yards of this and fifty yards of that. Oh, and I'll have a hundred yards of this glorious silver ribbon! It's just like moonlight. And send a hundred yards of this pink ribbon, please too, and I'll have a ribbon archway with mauve lamps made, leading from the palace to the wood. The queen will be delighted!'

'Certainly!' answered the witch, feeling excited to

think of all the gold she would get for such a lot of ribbon. 'The pink ribbon is very expensive, Your Highness. It's made of pink sunset clouds mixed with almond blossom. I've only just got a hundred yards left!'

'That will just do,' said the chancellor, getting up to go. 'Send it all to the palace, please. And don't forget the *pink* ribbon; it's most important, *most* important!'

And off the chancellor went to his carriage again.

Mother Ribbony Rose, who cared for gold more than she cared for anything else in the world, rubbed her hands together with delight.

'Now then, Pinkity!' she called. 'Come here and roll up all this ribbon I've been showing to the chancellor, and measure out all that he wants!'

Pinkity began rolling up the ribbon. He did it as quickly as ever he could, but even then it took him a long time. He measured out all the many yards that the chancellor wanted, and folded them neatly. Then he got some paper and began to make out the bill.

'Hallo,' said Pinkity, 'the inkpot's empty. I must

get the ink bottle down and fill it!'

He climbed up to the shelf where the big bottle of black ink was kept, and took hold of it.

But alas! Poor Pinkity slipped, and down fell the big bottle of ink on to the counter, where all the chancellor's ribbon was neatly folded in piles! The cork came out, and before Pinkity knew what was happening all the ink upset itself on to the lovely ribbon, and stained it black in great patches.

In came old Mother Ribbony Rose.

'Pinkity! Pinkity! Look what you've done! And I haven't any more of that pink ribbon! You did it on purpose, I know you did, you naughty, naughty little gnome!' stormed the witch, stamping up and down.

Pinkity was dreadfully frightened. He was so frightened that, without thinking what he was doing, he jumped clean through the window and ran away!

He ran and ran and ran.

Then he lay down beneath a hedge and rested. Then he ran and ran and ran again, until it was night.

At last he came to a beautiful garden, lit by

the moon, and quite empty, save for lovely flowers. It was the queen's garden, but Pinkity did not know it.

'I'm free! I'm free!' cried Pinkity, throwing his hat in the air. 'There's a dear little hole beneath this rock. I'll hide there, and I'll *never* go back to Mother Ribbony Rose.'

He crept beneath the rock, shut his eyes and fell fast asleep.

Next morning he heard fairies in the garden, and they were all talking excitedly.

'Yes, it was a naughty little gnome called Pinkity, who spoilt all the queen's lovely ribbon,' said one fairy.

'Yes, and he did it on purpose, old Mother Ribbony Rose says. Just fancy that!' said another.

'And the chancellor says if anyone catches him, they're to take him to the palace to be punished, and given back to Mother Ribbony Rose,' said a third.

Pinkity lay and listened, and felt the tears rolling down his cheeks. He had so hoped that perhaps the fairies would help him.

All that day Pinkity hid, and at night he crept out into the lovely garden, and the flowers gave him nectar to eat, for they were sorry for him.

For a long time Pinkity hid every day and only came out at night. One day he heard a group of fairy gardeners nearby, talking hard.

'What *are* we to do about those little ferns?' they said. 'Directly they come up, their tiny fronds are spread out, and the frost *always* come and bites them, and then they look horrid. It's just the same with the bracken over there!'

'It's so difficult to fold the fronds up tightly,' said the fern fairies. 'They *will* keep coming undone!'

'Well, we *must* think of something,' said the gardeners decidedly. 'The queen simply loves her fernery, and she will be so upset if the frost bites the ferns again this year. Let's go and ask the rose gardeners if they can give us any hints.'

That night Pinkity went over to the baby ferns and bracken and looked at them carefully. It was a very frosty night, and they looked very cold and

pinched.

'*I* know! I know!' cried Pinkity, clapping his hands. 'I'll *roll* them up like ribbons, and then they'll be quite warm and safe, and won't come undone till the frost is gone!'

So Pinkity started rolling each fern frond up carefully. It wasn't as easy as rolling ribbon, for the fronds had lots of little bits to tuck in, but he worked hard and managed it beautifully. The baby ferns were very grateful, and so was the bracken.

'Thank you, thank you,' they murmured. 'We love being rolled up, and we're much warmer now.'

Pinkity worked all night, and just as daylight came, he finished the very last piece of bracken and ran back to his hole to hide.

At six o'clock along came the gardeners. They stared and stared and stared at the ferns.

'Whatever has happened to them!' they cried in amazement. 'They're rolled up just like ribbon!'

'What a splendid idea!' said the head gardener. 'But who did it? Someone very kind and very clever must have done it!'

'*Who* did it? *Who* did it?' cried everyone.

Pinkity, trembling with excitement, crept out of his hiding place.

'If you please,' he said, '*I* did it!'

'Why, Pinkity! It's Pinkity, the naughty little gnome!' cried the fairies.

'I wasn't really naughty,' said Pinkity. 'The ink spilt by accident on the ribbon. I wouldn't have spoilt the dear queen's ribbon for anything in the world.'

'Well, you've been so kind to our ferns,' said the fairies, 'that we believe you. But how *did* you learn to be so clever, Pinkity?'

'I'm not clever *really*,' said Pinkity, 'but I can roll up ribbons nicely – it's the only thing I *can* do – so it was easy to roll up the ferns.'

The fairies liked the shy little gnome, and took him in to breakfast with them. In the middle of it in walked Her Majesty the queen.

'*Who* has looked after my baby ferns?' she asked in a pleased voice.

'Pinkity has! Pinkity has!' cried the fairies,

pushing Pinkity forward. Then they told the queen all about him.

'It was quite an accident that your lovely ribbon was spoilt,' said Pinkity, 'and I was dreadfully sorry, Your Majesty.'

'I'm quite *sure* it was an accident,' said the queen kindly, 'and I have found out that all Mother Ribbony Rose cares about is gold, so I am sending her right away from Fairyland, and you need never go back!'

'Oh, how lovely!' cried Pinkity joyfully.

'Your Majesty! Let him look after the ferns and bracken, and teach other fairies how to roll up the baby ones!' begged the fairies. 'He *is* so clever at it.'

'Will you do that for us, Pinkity?' said the queen.

'Oh, Your Majesty, I would *love* it!' answered Pinkity joyfully, feeling happier than ever he had been in his life before.

He began his work that very day, and always now you will find that fern fronds are rolled up as tight as can be, just like the ribbon Pinkity rolled up at the ribbon shop.

As for old Mother Ribbony Rose, she was driven right away from Fairyland, and sent to live in the Land of Deep Regrets, and nobody has ever heard of her since.

# Faraway Lands

# THE LAND OF BLUE MOUNTAINS

LITTLE Princess Lucy was crying in a corner of the royal nursery. She was so unhappy that her tears made a shiny puddle on the carpet.

'Why are you crying, Princess Lucy?' said her old nurse, ready with a big clean handkerchief to wipe away all her tears.

'I am crying because the queen, my mother, has been ill for weeks now, nurse,' wept Lucy. 'I cannot bear to see her so pale and thin. Why doesn't the doctor cure her?'

'Her illness cannot be cured by a doctor,' said the old nurse sadly. 'A spell has been cast upon her, a spell that was cast before my very eyes!'

'Tell me what you saw,' said Lucy who was now weeping faster than ever.

'I saw a little man from the Land of Blue Mountains,' said the nurse. 'He passed me as I lit the lamp outside your mother's bedroom. He slipped into her room and asked her for her wonderful jade necklace. She would not give it to him so, before he left, he muttered some magic words. It was a spell I am sure! The next day she fell ill, and has never left her bed since.'

'Oh, nurse!' said the Princess Lucy in dismay. 'Why should he put a spell on my mother?'

'The jade necklace came from that mysterious land,' said the nurse. 'And it is said that the little man who sold it to your father, the king, has always longed for it back.'

'If only my father was home!' said Lucy with a sigh. 'But he is far away, exploring new lands. Who

272

else can help my mother, nurse?'

'No one,' said the nurse. 'None would dare to go to the Blue Mountains save your father.'

'Where is the Land of Blue Mountains?' asked Lucy. 'Tell me.'

'Come with me, and I will show you,' said the nurse. So Lucy followed her up hundreds of stairs until she reached the highest room in the palace. It was a little round room with one tiny round window set in the western wall.

'Look through that window,' said the nurse. 'It is the only window in the palace that looks upon that strange land.'

Lucy saw a glorious sight. Far away rose peak upon peak of deep blue mountains, their summits tipped with gold in the setting sun. White clouds floated round the blue mountainsides, and the valleys between were dark purple.

It was so strange and wonderful that Lucy longed to go there. She looked for a long time until her nurse grew tired of waiting, and told her it was time for bed.

*If I went there, I might find the little man who put the spell on my mother*, she thought, as she climbed into bed. But when she asked how to get there, her nurse said, 'Nobody knows but your father. It is a cold, stony land, and the people there have hearts as cold and stony as their mountains. Now go to sleep, Lucy, and forget all you have seen.'

But in her dreams Lucy dreamt that she was following a little bent-over man up a blue mountainside, calling to him to stop. She dreamt that she came to a well full of gleaming, golden water. And last of all she dreamt that her mother was well again.

When she woke up, the dawn was just creeping in from the eastern sky. Lucy put on her bedroom slippers and ran up to the highest room in the palace. Once more she peeped through the tiny round window and saw the gleaming blue mountains.

But how strange! They seemed much nearer than the night before, and a broad road ran to them from the edge of the palace gardens.

In an instant Lucy had made up her mind. She

275

would go to the Blue Mountains herself. Quickly she ran to her room and dressed. Then she went downstairs and opened the garden gate. There lay the road, gleaming like gold in the morning sun. She stepped out on to it, and as she did so, she heard a bark behind her.

It was Saxon, her dog. He had heard her footsteps and had come to join her. Lucy was so pleased to see him.

'Oh, Saxon,' she said. 'Will you come with me to the Land of Blue Mountains?'

Saxon licked her hand, and then knelt down beside her. He wanted her to climb on to his broad back, for he often gave the little princess a ride.

'Oh, that is a splendid idea!' cried Lucy. 'Now we shall soon be there!' So off they went down the gleaming golden road, with the tall blue mountains shining far away in front of them, and the palace slowly growing smaller and smaller behind them.

After some time they came to a clear stream at the roadside, and they both drank from it. Then suddenly the dog gave a loud bark and pointed with

276

his paw to the road behind them.

Lucy looked – and what a strange sight she saw. The road was disappearing!

'Oh, the road is going!' she cried to Saxon. 'Quick! We must reach the Land of Blue Mountains before the road is quite gone!'

Off they raced, while behind them the road gradually disappeared as if someone were rolling it up. Great rocks and thick woods sprang up where the road had been. Faster and faster galloped the panting dog, and nearer and nearer came the mountains. 'Go on, go on!' cried Lucy. 'The road is almost gone behind us. It is disappearing as fast as we are galloping!'

She looked ahead and saw that they were very near the mountains. One of them, a tall spire of a mountain, had a great gate at its foot, and Lucy guessed it was the entrance to the land. Just as they reached it, the last piece of road disappeared, and the princess and the dog found themselves standing on a rocky piece of ground outside the gate. All around them stretched dark woods and

277

black rocks. The golden road was quite gone.

The gate swung open and they passed through together. Blue mountains towered up on every side. Their sides were bare and stony, and as blue as forget-me-nots. The little streams that fell down the sides were blue too, and the only plants that grew there were great bright blue things as large as saucers.

'What a strange country!' whispered Lucy and Saxon licked her hand gently to stop her from feeling afraid.

They chose one of the paths that led between the mountains and followed it. Lucy was surprised to see no one about – but at last she spied two little figures, and she called to them. They stopped and looked at her in astonishment.

As she drew near she saw that they were dressed in blue wool, and had woollen caps on their heads. Their eyes were cold and blue, and Lucy did not like them.

'What are you doing here?' the little folk demanded. 'Aren't you cold without a coat?'

'Not at all!' said Lucy in surprise. 'The sun is very warm. You must be hot in all those clothes.'

'Only those with warm hearts can keep warm here,' said one of the little men. 'We folk of the Blue Mountains are cold, even on the hottest day. Why did you come here?'

'I came to find the little man who put a spell on my mother,' said Lucy. 'He once sold a jade necklace to my father, the king.'

'That must be Blizzard, who lives at the top of this path,' said the little folk. 'But be careful of him. He is the coldest one of all.'

Lucy said goodbye and took the narrow path they pointed out to her, which led up the steep mountainside.

'I am so hot I don't know what to do,' said Lucy after a while. 'However can these people here be cold when they have all these mountains to climb!'

Just then a little bent-over man came toiling up another path nearby. Lucy called to him, but his sheepskin cap was pulled so firmly over his ears that he did not hear her.

'Perhaps that is Blizzard,' she said to Saxon. 'Come on. We'll follow him.'

So on they went, following the little blue man up the great blue mountainside. At last he went inside a small cottage set into the hillside. Lucy and Saxon followed, and knocked loudly.

Blizzard came to the door in surprise. Not many visitors came to his cottage.

'What do you want?' he asked.

'I am Princess Lucy and I have come to ask you to lift the spell from my mother,' said Lucy. 'You have made her ill, and I want her well again.'

Blizzard's eyes were like two shining sapphires.

'You have come to this cold, stony country,' he said, 'where we all shiver and freeze, and yet you have no coat and no hat. Let me feel your hand. Why, it is warm as fire!'

'And yours is as cold as ice,' said Princess Lucy with a shiver.

'It is cold as my heart,' said Blizzard mournfully. 'All people with cold hearts are sent to live here, and we never feel warm. If only I had a warm heart like yours! How happy I should be!'

'Yes and you would be kind too,' said Lucy. 'It was cruel of you to put a spell on my poor mother. Tell me how to undo it.'

'Why should I?' said Blizzard, his little cold eyes gleaming like ice. 'You have nothing to give me in exchange.'

Lucy began to cry. Her tears fell down her cheeks, and Blizzard touched them in wonder.

'Why, even your tears are warm,' he said. 'I would give anything to have a heart as warm as yours!'

'Then take that horrid spell off my mother and I will give you my warm heart and take your cold one!' said the little princess bravely.

Blizzard could not believe his ears at first, but as soon as he knew that Lucy meant what she said he took her by the hand and hurried her down the mountainside.

'We will go to the well of golden water,' he said. 'A bottle of that will cure your mother. Then we will go to the ice maiden who lives at the top of the highest mountain and she will change our hearts for

281

us. Oh, I shall be so happy when I get your warm heart for my own!'

Lucy hurried after him. On and on they went, until they came at last to the foot of a towering blue mountain, the highest of all, and at the very top was a shimmering palace of blue ice. They started up the winding path that led to the top and had not been climbing long before they came to a well, the same one that Lucy had seen in her dream. She looked down and saw golden water at the bottom. There was no bucket to send down, and Lucy wondered how they were to get the magic water. But the little man soon showed her.

He tied a rope round himself, knotted one end to a post of the well, and then let himself down to the water. He filled a bottle, and then, with Lucy's help, pulled himself up again. Where his clothes had touched the water he shone like the sunset. He gave the bottle to Lucy, who slipped it into her pocket.

Lucy felt a tug at her dress, and saw Saxon looking at her. He wanted her to climb on his back and run away without giving her warm heart to the little

282

blue man. But she would not.

'No, Saxon,' she whispered in his ear. 'A princess cannot break her promise.'

On they went to the shimmering blue palace and passed through a gate of blue sapphire so beautiful that it hurt Lucy's eyes to look at it. Then into a great hall they went, and the little princess saw a giantess sitting on a throne of silver.

'What do you want?' asked the ice maiden, and her voice sounded like ice cracking on a pond.

'This princess is going to give me her warm heart in exchange for my cold one,' said Blizzard. 'Will you make the magic that will change our hearts?'

'Why do you want a warm heart?' asked the ice maiden. 'Warm hearts are a nuisance. They make their owners do kind and unselfish deeds. It is much nicer to be cold and selfish.'

'But her tears are warm!' cried Blizzard. 'It must be wonderful to have warm tears and a warm heart to match!'

The giantess laughed, and it was like a shower of hail falling on a glass roof.

'If you wish it, I will change your hearts,' she said. 'You must hold hands and walk together to the gateway of our land. Kiss her twice when you get there, and look deep into her eyes. Then you will have her heart and she will have yours.'

'Thank you,' said Blizzard, and they left the palace with Saxon following behind. Down the mountainside they went, holding hands, and as they went Lucy's hand became cold, and Blizzard's became warm.

For a long time they walked, until at last they reached the gate through which the princess and her dog had passed that very morning. It was dusk now, and the moon was rising. For a minute it went behind a dark cloud. Blizzard let go of Lucy's hand, and waited for the moon to come out again. But before it did so, he felt two kisses, and found himself looking into two eyes, while two hands rested on his shoulders.

Suddenly there came a pain in his heart and it became warm. Blizzard felt so glad that the tears poured down his cheeks and he could not see.

'My heart is warm, my heart is warm!' he cried. 'I shall never be cold again! I am happy, happy, happy!'

He slipped through the gates and ran back to the Land of Blue Mountains, leaving Lucy standing alone very much astonished.

'But how can your heart be warm?' she called. 'You didn't kiss me, nor look into my eyes! My heart is not cold. It is as warm as ever.'

But there was no answer. Blizzard had gone.

Then Lucy felt a wet nose against her arm, and guessed what had happened. Saxon had pretended to be her when the moon had gone behind that dark cloud! He had stood up in front of Blizzard with his paws on the little man's shoulders, and had licked him twice!

'Oh, dear, kind Saxon, you have given up your own warm heart in place of mine!' cried Lucy, hugging him. 'I think you are the most wonderful dog in the world! But what has happened to Blizzard's cold heart? Have you got it?'

Saxon mournfully nodded his head. Then, very

sadly he trotted down the road beside the princess. His heart was heavy and cold, and he felt strange and unhappy. But he also felt glad because he had saved Lucy's warm heart for her, and she had the bottle of golden water safe.

The road spread out in front of them once more and they set off towards the moonlit palace, which was shining in the distance. It was dawn by the time they arrived and Lucy ran through the sleeping rooms to her mother's bedside. She poured the golden water into a glass and gave it to her mother to drink.

The queen sat up with a cry.

'The spell is gone!' she said. 'I am better! Oh, Lucy, tell me where you got the golden water from!'

Lucy told her story, and at the end the queen cried to think of poor Saxon and his cold heart.

'See him sitting by the fire, shivering,' said Lucy. 'What can we do for him, Mother?'

Just then the old nurse came into the room and cried out in delight to see Lucy, and to find the queen better once more. When she heard about

the poor dog, she smiled.

'Don't fret,' she said. 'His heart will soon be better. No dog can possess a cold heart for long. Feed him on milk mixed with your tears for him, and his heart will be as warm as ever in a few days!'

And so his heart gradually became warmer, and his bark became happier and happier, until at last his heart was as warm as ever. The Princess Lucy was so grateful that she had a fine collar made for him, and from it she hung a tiny golden heart. He will show it to you if ever you see him!

# YOU SIMPLY NEVER KNOW!

WILLIAM had a lovely new kite. He was very proud of it indeed. It had a beautiful tail, and it looked as if it would fly very well indeed.

'I do so hope I don't lose it,' said William to his mother, the first day he took it out to fly. 'It's a big kite – and the wind's so strong it might break the string.'

'Oh, I don't think so, dear,' said Mother. 'But, anyway, couldn't you just write your name and address on the kite? Then if it *does* fly off and somebody finds it, there's a chance they might be honest and bring it back.'

William thought that was a very good idea. He scribbled his name and address on the kite as neatly as he could.

The kite certainly flew well. It leapt up into the air at once, and tugged and pulled like a live thing.

William shouted loudly. 'Here we go! Pull, kite, pull! That's right – go higher and higher! See if you can catch that cloud!'

The kite flew very high. It almost seemed as if it *was* trying to catch a cloud. William began to find it rather hard to hold the kite. It made him run a few steps!

'Hey, kite! Don't pull me so!' he cried. But the kite flew with the wind and dragged William along again. He came to the stream and fell in! To save himself he let go of the kite string – and away went the kite on its own in the windy sky. It chased the birds. It flew through a cloud. It even raced after an aeroplane.

When William picked himself up, soaked from head to foot, he was cross and upset. 'Look at that! I've fallen into the stream, and I've lost my new kite. The very first time I flew it too! Thank goodness I put my name and address on it. Perhaps it may be brought back.'

Now the kite flew for miles and miles. It flew over a great wood at last, and then bumped into an enormous tree – a tree that grew so high it touched the clouds.

It was the Faraway Tree, of course, that stood in the middle of the Enchanted Wood. It banged against Moonface's door and lay still outside, tired out.

'Come in!' cried Moonface, thinking the bang was a knock. Nobody came in, of course, so Moonface opened the door. He was most astonished to see a kite there.

'What do *you* want?' he said, and picked it up. 'What a beauty you are! Hallo – there's a name and address written here. "William Wilson, Redroofs, Limming Village." Do you mean to say you've come all that way?'

The kite wagged its tail. Moonface called down the Faraway Tree. 'Hey, Saucepan Man, are you there? Look what's come to see me!'

Saucepan looked, clanking as he came up to see. He was all hung around with kettles and saucepans.

'Have to take it back,' he said, when he saw the name and address. 'Come along. We'll go now. The boy it belongs to will be very upset if he thinks he has lost it.'

The kite was too big to go down the Slippery-Slip that ran from the top of the Faraway Tree to the bottom in the very middle of the great trunk. So Moonface walked out on to a broad branch with Saucepan, and threw the kite into the wind. It rose into the air at once, and Moonface and Saucepan hung on to the tail.

The kite took them gently down to the ground. Their weight was too much for it to fly away. Moonface picked up the kite and tucked it under his arm. It was really far too big to go there, and looked very peculiar. Saucepan carried the tail. The string ran on the ground like a long pale worm

wriggling in and out.

Through the Enchanted Wood they went and over the ditch that surrounded it. Then they set off to catch the bus that went in the direction of Limming Village. The conductor said that the kite would have to go on top. It was an open-roofed bus so that was all right. Saucepan kept tripping over the tail as they went up the stairs, but at last they were safely sitting on top of the bus with the kite standing quietly beside them.

It was six o'clock before they arrived at Limming Village, and beginning to get dark. Moonface asked where Redroofs was, and then the two of them set off to take the kite to William.

They went to the back door, because they didn't think it was right to take kites to the front door. They knocked and William's mother opened the door.

She didn't see the kite at first. She only saw Moonface's shining round face and Saucepan all hung round with pans, wearing the usual saucepan for a hat.

'What a time to come selling kettles and saucepans!' she said crossly. 'No, I don't want any.'

'But look – we've brought back—' began Moonface, tugging at the kite.

'So *you've* got something to sell too,' said William's mother. 'I don't want anything at all. I don't buy at the door. Go away, please.'

She shut the door. Moonface and Saucepan looked at one another.

'I suppose we do look a bit peculiar to her,' said Moonface. 'We forgot that. We'd better just scribble a message on the kite, leave it here and go. After all, probably William's mother has never even heard of us.'

So they scribbled a message on the kite, set it down near the kitchen door, gave a loud knock and went down the path.

It was William who opened the door this time – and the first thing he saw was the kite!

'Mother! My kite – look! Somebody's brought it back!' he cried. 'Who was it, do you suppose? Has anyone been to the door?'

'Dear me, yes – I wonder if *they* brought it back,' said his mother. 'Two most peculiar-looking people came – one with a round shining face, and one all hung about with pans and kettles.'

'Mother!' said William. 'Oh, Mother – could it have been – no, of course it couldn't.' And then he saw the message scribbled on the kite.

Dear William,
Your kite fell in the Faraway Tree,
so we brought it back. It's a beauty.
Yours with love,
Moonface and Saucepan

'It was, it was!' shouted William. 'Mother, which way did they go? Mother, I simply *must* find them. Don't you realise who they were – they're Moonface and Saucepan, from the Faraway Tree. Which way did they go?'

But his mother didn't know. William set off down the path, looking all about in the half-darkness.

He heard a clanking noise some way down the road. That must be old Saucepan! He flew down the road after the noise.

The noise had gone round a corner. William rushed round at once. He could see something in the darkness not far off. 'SAUCEPAN!' he yelled. 'MOONFACE!'

The noise stopped. William rushed on eagerly.

'Wait for me, wait!' he cried, and at last he caught up with the noise, which had not begun again.

But what a dreadful disappointment! It was only Jim the farmer's boy going home on Cobber the horse, whose harness was jingle-jangling all the time. It had sounded exactly like the noise old Saucepan's kettles and pans made.

I wish I could tell you that William found Moonface and Saucepan. But he didn't. They were gone, and he could have wept. What a chance, what a wonderful, marvellous chance – and he had missed it. Poor Mother – she would be disappointed too, when she knew.

All the same, he was lucky, wasn't he? His kite had been brought safely back, he had had Moonface and Saucepan at his back door – and he's *still* got the little scribbled message on the kite. But, oh, what a pity he *just* missed his two Faraway Tree visitors.

# THE BED THAT RAN AWAY

ONCE upon a time there was a small girl called Anna and a little boy called Guy. Guy was a wide-awake little fellow. But Anna – dear me, what a sleepyhead she was!

She would not wake up in the morning! She was always yawning, all the day long, and she was always ready to go to bed at night.

Her mother used to get very tired of trying to wake her up each morning. She would go into Anna's room and say, 'Anna. Wake up! Time to get up!'

No answer from Anna.

'ANNA! WAKE UP! You'll be late for school!'

'M-mm-m-mm,' Anna would mumble, half asleep. Then her mother would pull all the clothes from her and cry, 'You lazy little girl! Get up, I say!'

Then she would go from the room, and that lazy little Anna would pull up the clothes again and go to sleep once more! So she hardly ever had time for a proper breakfast, and was always late for school.

One day her mother was so cross that she said she couldn't be bothered to wake up Anna any more.

'You can wake her up, Guy,' she said. 'Do what you like – squeeze a cold sponge over her head, take off the blankets and put them on the other side of the room – but wake her up.'

So Guy said he would – but dear me, it was difficult, because Anna could sleep even though cold water was pouring over her face, and when she found that her bedclothes were on the other side of the room, why, she just went to sleep again without

them, curling up her toes inside her nightdress for warmth. She was a sleepyhead!

Now one of Guy's schoolfellows had a grandmother who was supposed to be a very wise woman. She often went out in the early mornings and picked strange herbs and leaves to make potions. She was a kindly old woman, always ready to help anyone, and Guy wondered if she would be able to tell him how to cure Anna of her sleepiness.

So one evening he went to call on her. She lived in a little cottage on the edge of the wood. The old dame opened the door herself and smiled at Guy.

'Hallo, young man, and what can I do for you?' she asked.

Guy told her his trouble and she listened with a twinkle in her eye.

'A sleepyheaded sister,' she said when he had finished. 'Well, we must certainly cure her, Guy, or she won't be a bit of use in the world.'

'Can you cure her?' Guy asked eagerly.

'I'm not quite sure,' said the old woman. She went to a drawer and opened it. In it were the strangest

things Guy had ever seen – peacocks' feathers, sparkling powders, small dolls like pixies, shining butterflies' wings neatly piled together and tiny bottles of bright-coloured liquids.

The old dame took up a small yellow box and opened it. Inside were a number of very tiny shining stars, glittering brightly.

The old woman shook three out into her hand. 'Now these,' she said, 'are supposed to be a sure cure for a sleepyhead. Put one under the pillow of a sleepy person and it is said he will be cured by the next day. If not, put a second under his pillow the next night and a third the following night. After that he will wake up early each morning and never be a sleepyhead again. But these little stars are very old and may have lost their power, so don't trust too much to them, Guy. They may be no use at all. But you can try them if you like.'

'Oh, thank you!' cried Guy. He took an empty matchbox from his pocket and slipped the three curious stars inside it. They shone strangely and seemed full of magic.

'What do they do to make the sleepyhead wake up?'

'Oh, it is said that the bed makes a curious creaking noise that frightens the person in bed so much that he wakes up at once!' said the old dame. 'You must watch and see what happens, Guy.'

Guy thanked the old lady and said goodbye, and ran home. What a secret he had! He took out the little stars and looked at them. Would they really be powerful enough to cure such a sleepy person as Anna? Surely a little creaking and groaning wouldn't wake her up.

'I think I shall put all three stars under her pillow,' decided the little boy. 'Then perhaps the bed will make such a loud noise that it will waken even Anna!'

So that night when Anna was fast asleep in bed Guy stole up to her and slipped all three of the little shining stars under her pillows. Then off he went to his own bed, and left his door open so that he could hear when Anna's bed began to creak and groan.

At five o'clock in the morning, when the sun was

just rising and all the world was golden, Guy woke up. Whatever was that noise? He sat up in bed and remembered. Ah, it was Anna's bed. How angry she would be to be wakened up at five o'clock!

He slipped out of his bed and ran to Anna's room. The little girl was lying fast asleep as usual – but the bed was behaving very strangely.

It groaned deeply. It creaked heavily. It tossed the mattress up and down as if it were trying to shake Anna out of bed. But she didn't move!

Guy stood and watched. It was a very strange thing to see. Then he saw something even stranger!

The bed lifted up one foot and pawed the floor with it like a horse! Guy didn't like that much. It seemed far too weird! Whatever would it do next?

It lifted up another foot and knocked on the floor with that too – and then, oh my goodness me, it began to move! Yes, it really did! It walked towards the door, creaking and groaning for all it was worth, putting out first one foot and then another, just as if it were a four-legged animal!

Guy tried to push the bed back into its place but

it tapped him smartly on the toe and made him jump. It pushed him away and squeezed itself through the door and then it jolted itself down the stairs! It made such a noise at the time, creaking like a dozen doors and grumbling to itself like a live thing. Guy didn't know what to do!

'Anna, Anna, wake up!' he cried. 'Your bed is walking away with you!'

'Mm-m-mm-m-mm,' said Anna in her sleep.

'Anna! Get up!' shouted Guy, trying to roll the little girl out of bed. But she only curled herself up all the more tightly and slept soundly. It was quite impossible to wake her.

Guy was just going to run and waken his parents when he saw that the bed was beginning to run! It had got down the stairs and somehow or other the front door had opened and now the bed was out in the street, running along. There was no time to get help! By the time he had wakened his mother the bed would be out of sight and nobody would know where Anna had gone! He must keep close to the bed, whatever happened. If only he could wake Anna.

The bed jogged on happily, creaking as it went. Guy ran after it, still in his pyjamas, for he had had no time to dress. It ran faster. Guy ran fast too. The bed made for a little lane and rushed down it, almost galloping, so that Anna was jolted up and down, but still she didn't wake. Guy tore after the bed. It turned a corner and Guy ran to the corner too – but when he got there the bed was gone.

'It's gone!' said Guy in horror. 'Where is it?'

There was no bed to be seen. It had vanished into thin air. Not a creak, not a groan was to be heard. Poor Guy! Tears came into his eyes but he wiped them away. Crying wouldn't help Anna. No, he must go straight to the old woman who had given him those little shining stars and see if she could tell him where the bed had gone.

So off he went and the old dame was most surprised to have such an early visitor. When she heard what had happened she sat down in amazement.

'You shouldn't have put all three stars under the pillow,' she said at last. 'Of course that would give the bed the power to run right away. One star just makes it want to go, and it creaks and groans because it can't – but three stars! Well, of course it would disappear!'

'But Anna didn't wake up,' said Guy in despair.

'She *must* be a sleepyhead!' said the old dame. 'Well, well, we must see what we can do. The bed has gone to the Land of Nod, you know. Perhaps if we go there we can manage to rescue Anna.'

'Oh, will you go with me?' asked Guy.

'Of course!' said the old dame. 'Come and sit on my knee in my big armchair and it will take us to the Land of Nod, where we can look for poor Anna.'

She sat down and Guy climbed up on to her knee. She began to tell him a story. It was a sleepy story and Guy, who was tired, gradually felt his head beginning to nod. He would soon be asleep. The chair began to rock, for it was a rocking chair. It rocked and rocked, and at last it rocked so hard that Guy opened his eyes in surprise.

And do you know, it wasn't a chair after all! It was a boat, rocking on a deep blue sea. He was

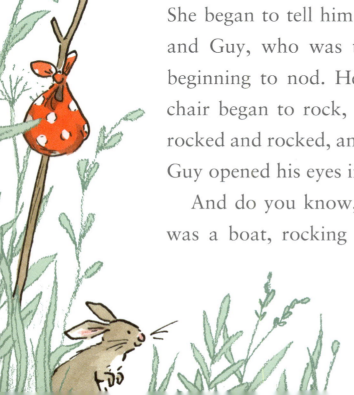

sitting on a soft cushion and the old dame was sitting opposite to him, smiling broadly.

'Well, here we are on the way to the Land of Nod,' she said. 'We shan't be long in this boat.'

The sea stretched for ever around them – or so it seemed. No land was in sight anywhere. Fish gleamed in the depths of the blue like stars. Guy wished he could catch some.

'We're nearly there,' said the old woman.

'Where?' asked Guy in surprise. He could see nothing at all but sea.

And then, to his enormous surprise, a curious, cloudy land seemed to rise out of the blue sea just by him. It grew bigger and bigger, and its towers shot up to the clouds and its palaces glimmered in the pale sunshine.

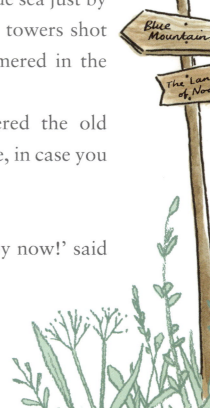

'That's the Land of Nod,' whispered the old woman. 'You mustn't make a noise here, in case you wake the sleepers.'

'Who are they?' asked Guy.

'Oh, I expect Anna is one of them by now!' said the old dame with a laugh.

The boat came softly to shore. The old dame got out and helped Guy to the sand. There was no wind, not a sound of any sort to be heard.

'It's just like a dream,' said Guy in a whisper.

'Well, you can only come here in a dream, you know,' said the old woman. 'Now we must see if we can find Anna.'

Nobody was in the blue misty streets. Guy's slippers seemed to make such a noise in that silent land.

Suddenly a white rabbit appeared, his long ears twitching forward. When he saw Guy and the old woman he ran silently towards them.

'Take off your shoes, boy,' he hissed. 'Don't you know that if you wake anyone in the Land of Nod a nightmare will gallop up and carry you away and you'll never be seen again?'

'Ooh!' said Guy in fright, taking off his slippers at once. He didn't want to be galloped off on the back of a nightmare!

The rabbit disappeared.

The old woman pointed silently to a big palace

308

not far off. 'That's where the sleepers are,' she whispered. 'Come on!'

They made their way to the palace. Its many pinnacles shone silvery in the early-morning light. There was a great flight of steps up to a wide glass door.

The little boy and the old woman went softly up – and just as they reached the top a sound came to their ears! It came from behind them. They turned to look.

And whatever do you think they saw? Why, Anna's bed coming slowly up the steps! Yes, they had got to the Land of Nod first!

The bed, creaking softly, and groaning under its breath, came up the steps one foot after another – and Anna still lay there fast asleep! Would you believe it?

The bed pushed open the shining glass door and went inside. The other two followed. What a strange sight met their eyes in the palace! There was a long hall and on either side were beds – some big, some small, but all with sleepers in curled up in slumber.

Anna's bed wandered down the hall, as if it were looking for a place. There was none for it, so it went through another door and into a smaller room. Beds were here too, but still there was no room. Into yet another room went the bed, groaning to itself as if it were very tired.

In this third room there was a space big enough for one more bed. Anna's bed walked carefully backwards into it and then, with a soft creak of delight, stood perfectly still. It had found its place in the Land of Nod!

'How can we wake her?' asked Guy in a whisper.

'You can't,' said the old woman. 'Nobody does anything but sleep here. We shall have to do the only thing we can – make the bed take her back home again.'

'But how can we do that?' asked Guy in surprise.

'If you can manage to take away the three little stars you put under Anna's pillow, I think the bed will have to go back,' said the old dame. 'It hasn't got rooted here yet, as all the others have. It has only just come. But I'm afraid it will be very angry.'

Guy slipped down the side of the bed. He put his hand under Anna's pillow and felt about for the three little stars. It really seemed as if they didn't want to be taken away for they ran about under the pillow like live things, and pricked Guy's hand whenever they could. But at last he got hold of them, slipped them into his matchbox and gave them to the old woman.

'Now we'll see what happens,' said the old dame. 'Stand back a little.'

As soon as the bed knew that the little magic stars were gone it began to make a terrible noise, for it knew it would have to go back to where it came from. It began to creak as loudly as twenty wardrobes, and groan so deeply that even Guy jumped. Then it moved! First one foot and then the other, but what a noise it made! It knocked here, it stamped there, it even seemed to dance with rage. Anna was shaken up and down but she didn't wake up! The bed moved out of its corner and went down the room. It ran out of the door, stamping and creaking like a mad thing.

Then, suddenly, the palace was full of strange horses with gleaming eyes and long tails. The nightmares had come! They stamped their hoofs, and raced about in anger. Guy felt frightened of them. He began to climb up on to a bed where a sleeper lay, lost in slumber – but the old woman pulled him off at once.

'You'll never go back home if you get into one of these beds!' she said. 'The only thing you can do is to catch a nightmare and ride it. It will take you home all right, though I warn you it will not be a pleasant ride.'

Guy did as he was told. He ran to one of the prancing coal-black nightmares and clambered on to its back. It threw up its head, made a whinnying noise and then galloped off at top speed. Guy clung on for all he was worth.

It was not a nice ride, as the old woman had said. The horse seemed to delight in giving poor Guy as many frights as it could. It galloped into a moonlit land and came to a high cliff. Far down below was the gleaming sea. The nightmare, instead of stopping at the edge of the cliff, jumped right over it!

Guy gave a gasp. Whatever would happen? Would they fall into the sea? But no! The horse stretched out its wings in mid-air and flapped safely back to the cliff edge, with Guy clinging tightly to its neck. It *hrrumphed* in delight when it saw how frightened Guy was.

Off it galloped again, and this time Guy saw a great wall in front of them. Surely the nightmare was not going to try to jump that! It would never get over the top.

But the horse gave a spring and up it went, with Guy wondering whatever would be on the other side. Over the top of the wall they went, and then Guy saw a swiftly flowing river on the far side of the wall. Splash! Into it they went, and the horse began to swim. Two or three times waves splashed over Guy's shoulders and he swallowed some water.

The nightmare scrambled out the other side and galloped off again with Guy almost tumbling off. It went so fast that the little boy's hair streamed out in the wind. Faster and faster – faster and faster

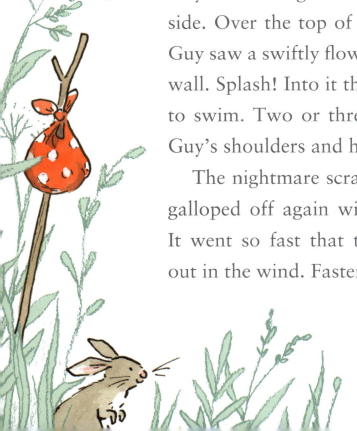

and faster! Guy clung on tightly. Goodness, surely the horse couldn't go much faster! Suddenly the animal put its hoof into a rabbit hole and over it went. Guy shot up into the air and came down again with a bump.

He gasped and opened his eyes.

And would you believe it? He was at home! By him was his bed, and he was on the floor.

*Well, anyone would think I had tumbled out of bed*, he thought, getting up. *Anyway, I'm safely back from the Land of Nod – but what about Anna?*

He ran to his sister's room – and was just in time to see the bed squeezing itself in at the door again, creaking and groaning. Anna was fast asleep, of course. The bed went to its place and stood perfectly still and silent. A clock downstairs struck seven.

His mother came out of her room.

'Hallo, Guy,' she said. 'Do try to get Anna down in time for breakfast today.'

Guy woke Anna up by pulling her out of bed and making her go bump on the floor. Then he sat down by her and told her all the extraordinary adventures

of that morning, and how she had been to the Land of Nod and back.

'Oh!' said Anna, turning pale. 'Do you know, I dreamt it too? I knew everything that happened, but I couldn't wake up. Oh, Guy, just suppose I'd stayed there!'

'Well, if I were you, I'd get up each morning as soon as you're called,' said Guy, 'just in case that bed of yours starts off again!'

'Oh, I will!' said Anna, and dressed in a hurry, anxious to get away from her peculiar bed. How surprised her mother was to see her down to breakfast ten minutes early!

The next morning, while Anna was still asleep, the bed creaked a little. My goodness, you should have seen Anna! She sat up in bed at once, leapt out and dressed as quickly as she could – and that bed has only got to give the smallest creak each day for Anna to be up and dressing in two shakes of a duck's tail!

'I'm not going to be taken off to the Land of Nod again!' she says – and I'm not surprised, are you?

# DICKIE AND THE WEST WIND

DICKIE'S mother was very unhappy. When Dickie came home from school she had tears in her eyes and she was hunting all over the place for something.

'What's the matter, Mummy?' asked Dickie in surprise, for he thought that grown-ups never cried.

'I've lost my lovely diamond ring,' said his mother. 'It's the one your daddy gave me years ago, and I love it best of all my rings. It was loose and it must have dropped off. Now I can't find it anywhere, and I'm so unhappy about it.'

'I'll help you to look for it,' said Dickie at once. 'Just tell me all the places you've been this morning, Mummy.'

'I had it on at breakfast time,' said his mother. 'Then I went to see old Mrs Brown who lives at the far edge of the meadow. I may have dropped it on my way there, of course. Perhaps you'd like to go and look on the path, Dickie?'

So off Dickie ran, his eyes looking all over the ground as he went. It was very windy, and the grass kept blowing about, which made it very difficult to see the ground properly. He soon came to the meadow and then he went down on his hands and knees and began to look very carefully indeed. He did so want to find that ring!

Suddenly he saw a small figure dart quickly behind a bush. It was too big for a rabbit and too small to be one of his playmates about to play a trick on him. What could it be? He peeped round the bush and what do you think he found hiding there?

318

It was a small elf with wide, frightened eyes and tiny, pointed ears! Now Dickie had never in his life seen an elf and he stared in surprise.

'Please don't hurt me!' said the elf in a little tinkling voice.

'Of course I won't!' said Dickie. 'But where are your wings? I thought all elves had wings and could fly.'

'Well, I usually *do* have wings,' said the little creature who was clothed in a beautiful suit of purple and blue. 'They are lovely silver ones, and I took them off this morning to clean them. I put them down on that bush there, and the wind came along and blew them away. Now I'm looking everywhere for them, but I can't find them anywhere. It's too awful!'

'I'm looking for something too,' said Dickie. 'I'm hunting for my mother's diamond ring. Have you seen it?'

'No,' said the elf. 'But I can easily get it for you, if you'll help me find my wings.'

'Could you really?' said Dickie excitedly. 'But

how am I to help *you*?'

'You could go to the West Wind and ask him what he's done with my wings,' said the elf. 'I can't do it myself because I'm afraid of him – he's so big and blustery – but you are big and tall so perhaps you wouldn't mind.'

*What an adventure this is turning out to be!* thought Dickie to himself, feeling more and more excited.

'Of course I will help you,' said Dickie to the elf. 'But wherever will I find the West Wind? I didn't even know it was a person!'

'Oh, goodness!' said the elf, laughing. 'He's very much a person, I can tell you. He's gone to see his cousin, the Rainbow Lady, on the top of Blowaway Hill.'

'Where's that?' asked Dickie. 'Tell me, and I'll go straight away.'

'Well, the quickest way is to find the tower in the wood,' said the elf, pointing down a little rabbit path through some trees. 'It has two doors. Go in the one that faces the sun. Shut it. Wish that

you could be in the same place as the West Wind. Open the other door and you'll find yourself there! Then just ask the West Wind what he's done with my wings and tell him he really must let me have them back.'

Dickie waved goodbye and ran off down the narrow little path. He had never been down it before. After a while he came to a tall, thin tower among the trees. Dickie walked all round it. It looked very strange indeed. There were no windows, but there were two small round doors. One faced the sun and the other was in shadow, just as the elf had described.

Dickie opened the sunny door and walked boldly through. The tower was high, dark and cold inside. Shivering, Dickie shut the door behind him and found himself in black darkness, just like night! He felt a little frightened, but he remembered what the elf had said and shouted, 'I wish I was on the top of Blowaway Hill.'

He heard a faint rushing sound and the tower rocked very slightly. Dickie opened the other door and daylight streamed into the strange tower,

making him blink. He walked out of the door – and *how* surprised he was!

He was no longer in the wood – he was on the top of a sunny hill, and in front of him was a small pretty cottage overgrown with honeysuckle.

*This must be the Rainbow Lady's house*, thought Dickie. He marched up the little path and knocked at the door. A voice called, 'Come in!' So Dickie turned the handle . . .

A draught of cold air blew on him as soon as he stepped inside. He shivered and looked around in surprise. Two people were sitting drinking lemonade at a little round table. A fire burnt brightly in one corner and a grey cat sat washing itself on the rug. Everything seemed quite ordinary until he looked at the people there!

One was the Rainbow Lady. She was very beautiful and her dress was so bright that Dickie blinked his eyes when he looked at her. She was dressed in all the colours of the rainbow, and her dress floated out around her like a mist. Her eyes shone like two stars.

The other person was the West Wind. He was fat and blustery, and his breath came in great gusts as if he had been running very hard. It was his breathing that made the big windy draughts that blew round the little room. His clothes were like April clouds and blew out round him all the time. Dickie was so astonished to see him that at first he couldn't say a word.

'Well! What do you want?' asked the West Wind in a gusty voice. As he spoke Dickie felt a shower of raindrops fall on him. It was very strange.

'I've come from the little elf who lives down in the meadow,' said Dickie. 'She says you took away her wings this morning, West Wind, and she does so badly want them back.'

'Dear me!' said the West Wind, surprised, and as he spoke another shower of raindrops fell on Dickie's head. 'How was I to know they belonged to the elf? I thought they had been put there by someone who didn't want them! I knew the red goblin was wanting a pair of wings so I blew them to him!'

'Oh dear!' said Dickie in dismay. 'What a pity!

The elf is really very upset. She can't fly, you see. She only took them off to clean them.'

'West Wind, you are always doing silly things like that,' said the Rainbow Lady in a soft voice. 'One day you will get into trouble. You had better go to the red goblin and ask for those wings back.'

'Oh, no, I can't do that,' said the West Wind, looking very uncomfortable and puffing more raindrops all over the room.

Dickie looked round to see if there was an umbrella anywhere. It was not very nice to have showers of rain falling all over him whenever the West Wind spoke. He found an umbrella in a corner and put it up over himself.

'Oh, yes, you *can* go and get the wings back,' said the Rainbow Lady, and she said it so firmly that the West Wind eventually agreed. He got up, took Dickie's hand and went sulkily out of the door. He had a very cold, wet hand, but Dickie didn't mind. It was very exciting.

The West Wind took Dickie down the hill at such a pace that the little boy gasped for breath. They

326

came to a river and the Wind jumped straight across it, dragging Dickie with him. Then he rushed across some fields and at last came to a small, lopsided house. A tiny goblin sat in the garden with a schoolbook, crying bitterly. The West Wind took no notice of the little creature but walked quickly up and knocked on the door.

'Stay here,' he said to Dickie, and left him in the garden. The little boy went over to the goblin.

'What's the matter?' he asked. The little goblin looked up. He had a quaint, pointed face and different-coloured eyes – one was green and the other was yellow.

'I can't do my homework,' he said. 'Look! It's taking-away sums and this one *won't* take away.'

Dickie looked – and then he smiled – for the silly little goblin had put the sum down wrong! He had to take 18 from 81, and he had written the sum upside down so that he was trying to take 81 away from 18. No wonder it wouldn't come right!

Dickie put the sum down right for him and the goblin did it easily. He was *so* grateful.

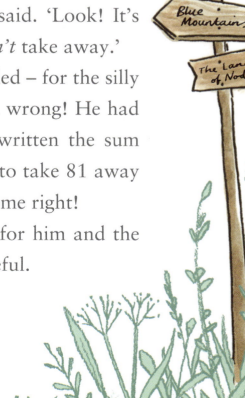

'Is there anything else I can help you with?' asked Dickie kindly.

'Well,' said the goblin shyly. 'I never can remember which is my right hand and which is my left, and I'm always getting into dreadful trouble at school because of that. I suppose you can't tell me the best way to remember which hand is which?'

'Oh, that's easy!' said Dickie at once. 'The hand you are *writing* with is your *right* hand, and the one that's *left* is the *left* one, of course!'

'Oh, that's wonderful!' said the little goblin in delight. 'I shall never forget now. I always know which hand I write with, so I shall always know my *right* hand and the other one *must* be the left. Right hand, left hand, right hand, left hand!'

Just at that moment the door of the little house flew open and out came the West Wind in a fearful temper.

'That miserable red goblin won't give me back those wings!' he roared, and a whole shower of rain fell heavily on poor Dickie and his new goblin friend. 'So we can't have them!'

Dickie stared in dismay. Now he wouldn't be able to take them to the elf and she wouldn't give him his mother's ring! It was too bad. He looked so upset that the small goblin he had just helped gently took hold of his hand.

'What's the matter?' he asked. 'Do you want those silver wings that the West Wind gave my father this morning? They were really for me to learn to fly on, but if you badly want them, you shall have them back. You've been so kind to me! I'd like to do something in return!'

'Oh, *would* you let me have the wings?' said Dickie in delight. The little goblin said nothing but ran indoors. He came out with a pair of glittering silver wings and gave them to Dickie. The little boy thanked him joyfully and turned to go. The West Wind took his hand and back they went to Blowaway Hill again.

'Well, you never know when a little kindness is going to bring you a big reward!' said the West Wind in a jolly voice. 'It's a good thing you helped that little goblin, isn't it?'

'Oh, yes,' said Dickie happily. 'Now I must get back to the meadow again and give these wings to the elf.'

But when he turned to look, he was dismayed to see that the tower had disappeared.

'Oh, no!' he cried. 'The tower has gone! However am I to get back home?'

Poor Dickie! It was quite true – the magic tower had gone and could not take him back to the wood as he had planned! But luckily the Rainbow Lady was watching through the window and came out to see what was wrong.

'Don't worry,' she said when Dickie explained what had happened. 'Just put on these elf wings, and the West Wind will blow you gently through the air back to the meadow.'

The Rainbow Lady took the wings from Dickie and clipped them neatly on to his shoulders.

'Now!' she said, turning to the West Wind. 'I said *gently*, so please don't be rough. Remember your manners for once!'

Then Dickie felt himself rising into the air, higher

330

and higher until he was far above the hill. His wings beat gently backwards and forwards and the West Wind blew him swiftly along. It was a most wonderful feeling.

'This is the most marvellous adventure I shall ever have!' said Dickie joyfully. 'Oh, how I wish I always had wings! It is lovely to fly like this!'

The West Wind smiled and remembered his manners and did not blow too roughly. Soon Dickie could see the meadow far below and the two of them started to glide gently downwards.

The West Wind said goodbye and left Dickie on the edge of wood. He soon found a path he knew and ran along to the bush where he had seen the elf. She was still there waiting for him. When she saw that he had her wings on his back she cried out in delight and ran to meet him.

She unclipped her wings from Dickie's shoulders and put them on her own. 'Oh, thank you, thank you!' she cried.

'Could you give me my mother's ring now?' asked Dickie. 'You said you would if I helped you.'

'Of course!' said the elf. 'While you were gone I set all the rabbits in the wood hunting for me – and one of them brought me this lovely shining ring. Is it your mother's?'

Indeed it was! So Dickie ran all the way home and when he showed his mother the ring she could hardly believe her eyes.

'You *are* clever to find it!' she said.

'I didn't find it – a rabbit found it,' said Dickie. But his mother didn't believe him, and when he told her his adventure she said he really must have been dreaming!

So next week he is going to ask that elf to come to tea with him – and then everyone will know it wasn't a dream! I wish I was going for tea with them too, don't you?

# IN NURSERY-RHYME LAND

BETTY and John had a lovely wallpaper in their playroom. It showed all the nursery-rhyme folk going about their work. There were Jack and Jill going up the hill, Tommy Tucker singing for his supper, Little Bo Peep looking for her sheep and many, many others.

Betty and John were never tired of looking at their wallpaper. There were trees and hills on it, and little round ponds with ducks. There were funny houses, and there was Noah's ark floating on a river, with Mr and Mrs Noah looking out of the window. A great many of the animals were peeping out of the top, and they all looked very happy. It really was a *lovely* wallpaper.

'Don't you wish we could visit the land on our wallpaper?' asked Betty one day. 'It does look so exciting, and we should be able to meet so many nursery-rhyme folk!'

John wished they could too, but he felt certain that they never would. Things like that never seemed to happen to people.

But one evening, as they were sitting by the fire reading a book, John happened to look up at the wallpaper – and he saw a very strange thing.

All the people on it were moving! Jack and Jill were really walking up the hill, Noah's ark was really floating along the river and Little Jack Horner was really eating his pie!

'I must be dreaming!' said John in the greatest surprise. 'I say, Betty! Look at the wallpaper! Does it seem different to you?'

334

Betty looked, and then she jumped to her feet in astonishment.

'Why, all the people are alive!' she cried. 'Oh, John! Let's call Mummy!'

'No, don't let's,' said John. 'The wallpaper would go quite ordinary again as soon as she came in. I know it would. Let's go nearer and look at it. Oh, Betty! Isn't it peculiar?'

The two children ran close to the paper, and looked at it. There was no doubt that everyone on it was moving.

'It doesn't look like a paper now,' said Betty. 'It looks like real land, only very far away. Oh, John, John! It's suddenly getting bigger!'

John caught hold of Betty's hand, and held it tight. Yes, everything in the paper was getting very large. Whatever was going to happen?

The two children stood quite still and stared hard. In front of them was a little house, and this seemed to be getting nearly as big as a real house. Soon it was so big that the children couldn't see anything else at all. It hid everything.

335

'John! It's not a paper house, it's *real*!' said Betty. 'Look, the chimney's smoking! Something very strange has happened. Oh dear, it's rather frightening – but isn't it *exciting*?'

'Where's the playroom?' said John, looking behind him. 'Why, Betty, it's gone! We're standing in the garden of the little house! It must be magic, really it must!'

Sure enough the playroom was gone. The children were standing on a tiny path in front of the little house they had so often seen on their wallpaper. They had wondered who lived there, for the door was shut, and there was no one looking out of the window.

'Well, we've often wanted an adventure, and now we've got one!' said John. 'Let's enjoy it, Betty!'

The sun was shining all around them, which was very strange, because it had been evening time in the playroom. It seemed about midday, and was very hot.

'We can't stand on this garden path all day,' said John. 'What shall we do, Betty?'

Just as he said that the door of the cottage opened,

336

and out came a little girl with a bowl of curds and whey in her hands.

'It's Little Miss Muffet!' said John in excitement. 'Now we know who lives in this cottage, Betty.'

'Good morning,' said Little Miss Muffet. 'What are you doing on my garden path? Did you want to see me?'

'No,' said John. 'We just found ourselves here. Please excuse us. We are very glad to see you.'

'That's nice of you,' said Miss Muffet. 'Come with me. I'll show you a dear little tuffet of grass that I always sit on every day to eat my curds and whey.'

She ran down the path and out of the gate. The two children followed her. She took them to a little wood, and there, under the trees, was a small grassy seat, just high enough for a little girl to sit on. Miss Muffet sat down, and smiled at Betty and John.

'Would you like to sit on it just for once?' she asked Betty. Betty said yes, she would love to. So down she sat, thinking what a dear little tuffet it was.

But suddenly John began to shout and scream.
'Get up, Betty! Quick, get up! Here's the spider!
Oh quick! It's the biggest I've ever seen!'

Betty jumped up in a dreadful hurry. Sure enough, letting itself down from a tree just over Betty's head, was a spider nearly as big as Betty herself! Miss Muffet screamed and ran away, leaving her curds and whey beside the tuffet. Betty ran too, and John caught hold of her hand and ran with her.

When they had run a long way, they turned and looked back. The spider was sitting on the tuffet, eating Miss Muffet's curds and whey!

'Just fancy that!' cried John. 'He does that every day, I expect. If I were Miss Muffet, I wouldn't go and sit on that tuffet any more, would you, Betty?'

'No,' said Betty with a shiver, for she didn't very much like spiders. 'Miss Muffet's gone, John. I expect she went back to her little house. Come on, let's go and find someone else.'

They went on down a little winding lane. Soon they came to a small boy sitting in a corner of a field eating a big pie. He had very bad manners, for instead of using a spoon, he put in his thumb and finger, and pulled the plums out with them.

'It's Little Jack Horner!' whispered Betty.

'What a good boy am I!' said Jack Horner, popping a great big plum into his mouth. 'Hallo, you two! Where are you going?'

'We don't know,' said John. 'We're just wandering about.'

'Oh, well, mind you don't get caught by the Old Woman Who Lives In A Shoe,' said Jack Horner, taking out another plum, and popping it into his mouth. 'She's lost some of her children, and she's out looking for them. If she catches you, you'll have a very bad time. She feeds them on broth without any bread, and whips them all soundly and sends them to bed.'

'Good gracious!' said John in alarm. 'Do you really think she would try to catch us, Jack?'

'Rather!' said Jack. 'She tried to get me yesterday, but I got the Cow With The Crumpled Horn to frighten her off. The old cow is a great friend of mine, you know. She lives in this field. Look, there she is.'

John and Betty looked. They saw a fat brown cow grazing nearby. One of her horns was all crumpled. She looked at them with her great eyes,

340

and then went on grazing.

'Hi! Look out! There's the old woman!' Jack Horner suddenly cried. John and Betty looked round quickly. They saw an old woman coming up the lane.

John caught hold of Betty's hand, and ran for his life. The old woman saw them, and at once began to run after them.

'Come here, you naughty children!' she cried. 'I've been looking for you everywhere. Come back to the shoe at once.'

Betty and John tore down the lane. They turned the corner, and came to a little cottage. The front door was open, so without thinking they ran into it, shut the door and then peeped out of the window. The old woman soon came by. She stopped at the gate and looked all about. John and Betty trembled – but she didn't come in. Instead she stood at the gate as if she was waiting for someone.

Soon that someone came. It was a little girl carrying a doll, and she came dancing to the gate and opened it. Then the old woman stretched out

her hand and took hold of her shoulder.

'You're one of my lost children!' she said in a very cross voice.

'Indeed I'm not!' said the little girl, tossing her head. 'I'm Mary Mary Quite Contrary, and this is my house and garden. Take your hand off me, old woman, and go away!'

'You rude little girl!' said the old woman. 'It will do you good to come and live in my shoe for a while. You shall come with me and learn manners!'

Mary began to cry, but it was no good. Off she had to go with the old woman. Betty and John looked on in dismay, very glad to think they had not been caught too.

'This must be Mary Quite Contrary's garden,' said John. 'Look, there are the silver bells hung on sticks, and all the beds are edged with cockle shells. But what are those dolls sitting out there?'

'Why, those are the pretty maids all in a row!' said Betty. 'Don't you remember the nursery rhyme, John?'

'Oh, yes,' said John. 'Well, come on, Betty.

We'd better leave here, and go on again. What an adventure this is!'

'I do hope we don't meet that horrid old woman again!' said Betty. 'I'd like to see Noah's ark, wouldn't you, John?'

'Yes,' said John. 'Let's ask the way to the river.'

So when they met Little Bo Peep looking for her sheep, they asked her the way, and she told them.

'You don't happen to have seen my sheep, do you?' she asked. 'I keep losing them, the naughty things.'

'No, we haven't seen any sheep at all,' said John. 'Only the Cow With The Crumpled Horn.'

On they went again, and soon came to the river. And there, floating on the water, was Noah's ark. Mr and Mrs Noah were looking out of the window, and all the animals were peeping out of the top, just as they had done in the wallpaper. But now they were very big, and the ark was like a great house.

'Good morning!' cried Mr and Mrs Noah. 'Do come in and see us! We'll send the hippo over to

you, and you can climb on his back. Then he will carry you across.'

All the animals began to bellow and roar, howl and bark, and Betty and John felt a bit frightened.

'I don't think we will, thank you,' said John. 'The animals don't seem to want us very much.'

'Bless you, that's only their way of saying "Do come!" said Mrs Noah. 'They won't hurt you.'

But the lion looked rather fierce, and John and Betty really thought that the ark was much too crowded for them to visit it. So they said no thank you again quite firmly, and then ran down the river path as fast as they could.

All the animals looked after them, and for a long time they made such a noise that John and Betty couldn't hear anything else. Soon they came to a little hill, and ran up the winding path to the top. Then who should they see coming down but Jack and Jill carrying a full pail of water between them.

Just as Jack and Jill came up to them, Jill tripped on a stone and over she went, dragging Jack with her. The pail spilt all its water, and Jack began to howl.

'Oh dear, I *thought* you'd fall over!' said Betty. 'You always do in our picture books. Never mind, get up and I'll bind your forehead with a nice clean handkerchief.'

She tied her handkerchief right round Jack's head and he soon stopped crying. Jill thanked Betty very much, and asked her where she was going. But before Betty could answer, Jack gave a yell.

'Look! There's the Old Woman Who Lives In A Shoe! Look out, or she'll catch us!'

At once Jack and Jill tore down the hill, and soon disappeared. John looked round and saw the old woman very near to them. Betty took hold of John's hand, and very quickly the two children ran away from her again.

But alas for them! The path they took led to the river! It ended there, and there was no other way out except by going into the water. Betty and John didn't know what to do. They saw Noah's ark away in the distance, but it was too far off to be of any help.

The old woman came panting after them. She took hold of their hands and held them tight.

'Why do you run away, you naughty children?' she scolded. 'I have been looking for you all morning.'

'We aren't your children,' said John. 'You must let us go.'

'*Must* indeed!' said the old woman. 'You are like Mary Quite Contrary. You need to learn manners. I've whipped her and put her to bed, the naughty little girl. Come along with me, and have your broth without any bread.'

Betty began to cry, and John to struggle, but it was no use. The old woman was just as strong as their father was and they couldn't get away. They had to go with her.

They saw Little Tommy Tucker singing for his supper, and Tom, Tom The Piper's Son, and Little Red Riding Hood on the way, but although John called to them to come and rescue them, they didn't do anything of the sort. They just ran away as fast as their legs could carry them.

Betty was still crying.

'Oh, John!' she said. 'Nursery-Rhyme Land would be lovely without the Old Woman Who Lives

In A Shoe. I do wish we were back in our own playroom, don't you?'

'Yes, I do,' said John. 'But it's no use wishing.'

But it *was* some use! No sooner had the two children wished their wish than something funny happened. The houses and fields began to get smaller and smaller, the paths narrower, and the people very tiny. Only the old woman seemed just as big as ever. She held them by the arms, and they couldn't get away.

Smaller and smaller grew Nursery-Rhyme Land – or was it that Betty and John grew larger and larger? They didn't know. Then suddenly it wasn't a land any more – but just a big flat stretch of wallpaper, with houses and fields, ponds, river and people painted on it. They were in their playroom!

But the old woman still held their arms tightly. Had she come to their nursery with them? John and Betty turned round to tell her that if she didn't let them go they would call for their mother.

And oh dear me, what a surprise! It wasn't the old woman after all, but Mummy herself, smiling

at them.

'Well, you've been standing looking at your wallpaper so long that I really thought you'd gone to sleep!' she said. 'Come along, my dears, it's bath time, and the water's lovely and hot.'

'Oh Mummy, we thought you were the Old Woman Who Lives In A Shoe!' said John. 'I'm *so* glad you're not!'

'Well, where did she go to?' asked Betty, staring at Mummy in surprise. 'She was here a minute ago.'

'Oh, so you *have* been asleep, then, and dreaming too!' laughed Mummy.

'No, we haven't, Mummy,' said Betty. 'We've been to the Nursery-Rhyme Land in the wallpaper, and we had the most exciting adventures!'

But Mummy wouldn't believe her, so Betty says that next time she goes, she will ask Mary Quite Contrary for a silver bell and a cockle shell from her garden – and then Mummy will know for certain it's all as true as true can be!

# ADVENTURES UNDER THE SEA

DICK was fast asleep one night when there came flying in at his bedroom window a fairy dressed in blue and green.

'Wake up, wake up!' cried the fairy.

Dick woke with a jump, and sat up.

'What do you want?' he asked.

'Are you the little boy who picked up a jellyfish that was lying in the sun and kindly put it into a pool again?' asked the fairy.

'Yes, I did, this morning,' answered Dick.

'Well, when it got back into its home, it found the king of the sea and asked if you might, for a treat, be taken under the sea to the sea fairies' home,' said the fairy.

'Oh, I'd *love* to come!' cried Dick.

'Come down to the seashore quickly then, just as you are,' said the fairy. 'I'll meet you there.'

Dick slipped downstairs, and was away on the beach ever so quickly. Across the water stretched a shimmering path of moonlight.

'Hold my hand,' said the sea fairy, 'and we'll run along the moon path.'

Dick didn't think it would hold him, but it did. And off the two went, running along the bright moon path over the waves.

At last they stopped. 'Now,' said the fairy, 'shut your eyes while I say some magic words to make you able to go down to my home.'

Dick shut his eyes, and the fairy sang some queer-sounding words. Dick felt himself sinking down and down and down.

350

'Oh,' he cried, when he opened his eyes, 'what a lovely place!'

He was standing in a great blue-green hall decorated with long streamers of waving seaweed. At one end sat Neptune, the king of the sea, with a crown of beautiful shells.

'Welcome!' he said. 'It isn't often I have a visitor from above the sea. Would you like to see some of the wonderful things here?'

'Oh, yes please,' said Dick.

Neptune turned to the blue and green fairy. 'Pearl,' he said, 'show Dick around our sea home.'

'Come along, Dick,' said Pearl.

'Dear me!' said Dick, staring at her. 'Whatever have you done with your legs, Pearl?'

'Oh, I only use legs for the land,' laughed Pearl. 'I put a tail on down here. Isn't it a nice one?' and off she swam, with Dick following.

They came to a dark, quiet cave, in which sat a solemn little merman with a long yellow tail. He had a silvery net, and was gazing up through the water.

'What's he doing?' asked Dick.

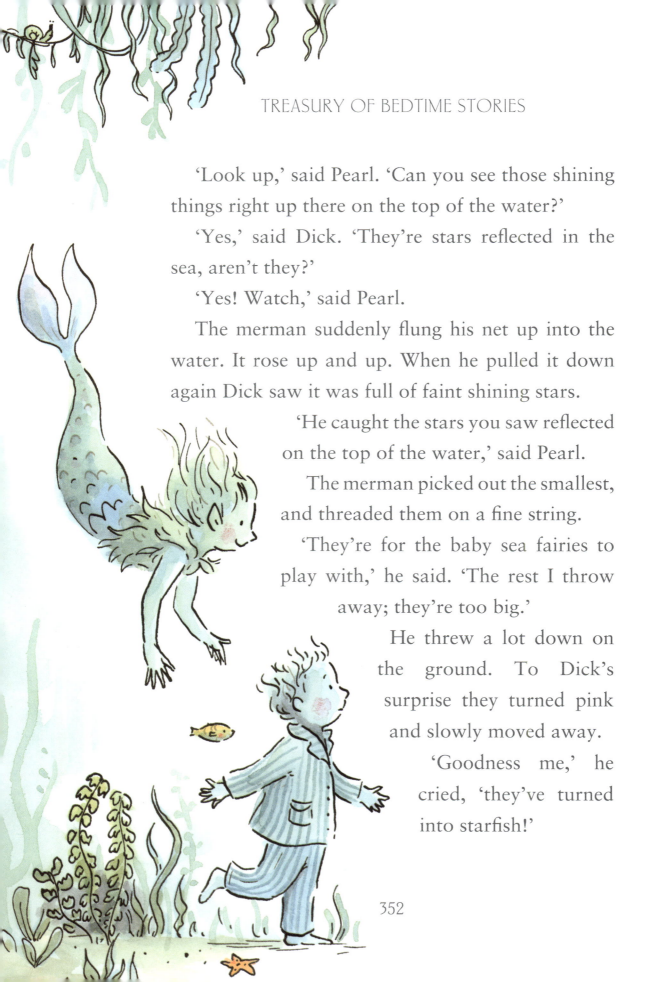

'Look up,' said Pearl. 'Can you see those shining things right up there on the top of the water?'

'Yes,' said Dick. 'They're stars reflected in the sea, aren't they?'

'Yes! Watch,' said Pearl.

The merman suddenly flung his net up into the water. It rose up and up. When he pulled it down again Dick saw it was full of faint shining stars.

'He caught the stars you saw reflected on the top of the water,' said Pearl.

The merman picked out the smallest, and threaded them on a fine string.

'They're for the baby sea fairies to play with,' he said. 'The rest I throw away; they're too big.'

He threw a lot down on the ground. To Dick's surprise they turned pink and slowly moved away.

'Goodness me,' he cried, 'they've turned into starfish!'

'Yes, they always do that,' answered Pearl. 'Now you know why they're shaped like stars. Come along!'

She took him out into a wide, open, sandy place, with rocks all around and beautiful sea flowers. Playing about were baby sea fairies, all with tails.

'Would you like to see them play their favourite game?'

'Yes, I would,' answered Dick.

Pearl went to a big square rock and opened the top, just like a box lid. All the baby fairies swam over to her, calling out, 'Our balloons, our balloons!'

'Oh, you're giving them jellyfish!' cried Dick in surprise.

'Yes, they're not like *your* balloons,' laughed Pearl, 'and they're made of jelly, so that they don't burst and frighten the babies.'

Dick watched the little fairies. Each held on to the streamers hanging down from the jellyfish, and away they floated, up and up, carried by their strange balloons.

'Oh,' cried a baby, tumbling down, 'mine is broken!' His jellyfish went sailing away by itself. Soon three or four more babies came tumbling down, laughing and rolling on the sand.

'There go their balloons!' cried Dick.

'Yes,' said Pearl, 'and I expect you'll find them floating about helplessly somewhere at the edge of the sea tomorrow with their strings hanging down.'

'I often wondered what use jellyfish were,' said Dick. 'I'm so glad I know now.'

'Now we'll go and see the white horses,' said Pearl, swimming off.

'Oh, are there *really* white horses in the sea?' asked Dick. 'I thought they were just white foam on the top of waves.'

354

'Dear me, no!' said Pearl. 'When they gallop along under the sea, and make big waves come, it's their curly white manes you can see peeping up here and there – not just white foam!'

'Oh, there they are!' cried Dick. There in front of him stretched a wide field of green seaweed, and munching it were great white horses with beautiful curly manes of snow-white.

'Stroke one,' said Pearl, 'they're quite tame.'

Dick stroked one, and it felt as soft as foam.

'I'm going to let one take you home,' said Pearl. 'Jump on his back.'

Dick climbed up.

'Goodbye!' called Pearl. 'I'm glad you came.'

'Goodbye!' shouted Dick, holding on to the thick mane of his horse as it galloped off.

When it got to the seashore it stood still. Dick slipped off and watched it disappear into the waves.

'*What* a lovely night I've had!' he said, as he ran back home again and cuddled down into bed.

# Acknowledgements

All efforts have been made to seek necessary permissions. The stories in this treasury first appeared in the following publications:

'Teddy and the Elves' was first published in Great Britain as a standalone novel in 1994.

'Corovell the Fairy' first appeared as 'The Fairy Dustman' in *Merry Moments*, Vol. 3, No. 152, 1922.

'Paddy-Paws and the Star' first appeared in *Sunny Stories for Little Folk*, No. 98, 1930.

'Morning Mist and Starshine' first appeared as 'The Fairy Queen's Frock' in *Merry Moments*, Vol. 4, No. 156, 1922.

'Connie's Curious Candle' first appeared in *Enid Blyton's Sunny Stories*, No. 194, 1940.

'One Rainy Night' first appeared in *Enid Blyton's Sunny Stories*, No. 229, 1941.

'The Tale of Twiddle and Ho' first appeared in *Sunny Stories for Little Folks*, No. 188, 1934.

'The Boy Who Turned Into an Engine' first appeared in *Enid Blyton's Sunny Stories*, No. 58, 1938.

'The Enchanted Slippers' first appeared in *Sunny Stories for Little Folks*, No. 191, 1934.

'The Sneezing Dog' first appeared in *Enid Blyton's Sunny Stories*, No. 343, 1944.

'Stamp-About's Spell' first appeared in *Enid Blyton's Magazine*, No. 14, Vol. 4, 1956.

'The Enchanted Doll' first appeared in *Sunny Stories for Little Folks*, No. 214, 1935.

'A Basket of Surprises' first appeared in *Sunny Stories for Little Folks*, No. 242, 1936.

'The Tale of Bushy the Fox' first appeared in *Sunny Stories for Little Folks*, No. 148, 1932.

'The Tale of Jig and Jog' first appeared in *Enid Blyton's Sunny Stories*, No. 43, 1937.

'Binkle's Wonderful Picture' first appeared in *The Enid*

# ACKNOWLEDGEMENTS

*Blyton Book of Bunnies*, 1925.

'The Adventures of the Toy Ship' first appeared in *Sunny Stories for Little Folks*, No. 170, 1933.

'The Gossamer Elf' first appeared in *Tales of Green Hedges*, 1946.

'Fireworks in Fairyland' first appeared in *The Teachers World*, Vol. 28, No. 932, 1922.

'The Rose that Didn't Grow' first appeared in two parts in *The Teachers World*, Vol. 28, Nos. 951 and 953, 1922.

'Muddy-One and Pranky' first appeared in *Tales of Green Hedges*, 1946.

'Pinkity and Old Mother Ribbony Rose' first appeared in two parts in *The Teachers World*, Vol. 29, Nos. 959 and 960, 1923.

'The Land of Blue Mountains' first appeared in *Sunny Stories for Little Folks*, No. 156, 1932.

'You Simply Never Know!' first appeared in *Enid Blyton's Sunny Stories*, No. 480, 1950.

'The Bed that Ran Away' first appeared in *Sunny Stories for Little Folks*, No. 217, 1935.

'Dickie and the West Wind' first appeared in *Sunny Stories for Little Folks*, No. 219, 1935.

'In Nursery-Rhyme Land' first appeared in *Sunny Stories for Little Folks*, No. 85, 1930.

'Adventures Under the Sea' first appeared as 'Under the Sea' in *Merry Moments Annual*, 1923.